## THE DARK FIGURE'S RIGHT HAND
## BECAME A THREE-CLAWED TRIDENT,

his thumb, fore and middle fingers
a trio of hooks. He swung this weapon up and
then down, the longer fingers ramming right through
the hitman's eyes and the thumb firmly
imbedded in the nasal passage up to the palm.
The pain was absolutely unbelievable
as blood poured from the hitman's ruined
eye sockets.

   Then, the hitman heard words which
seemingly came from inside his own brain. He felt he
could do nothing else but answer.


**"Who sent you?"** were the words. **"Who paid you?"**

Books by Wade Barker

*Ninja Master #1: Vengeance Is His*
*Ninja Master #2: Mountain of Fear*
*Ninja Master #3: Borderland of Hell*
*Ninja Master #4: Million-Dollar Massacre*

Published by
WARNER BOOKS

# NINJA MASTER

# #4

# MILLION-DOLLAR MASSACRE

## Wade Barker

**WARNER BOOKS**

A Warner Communications Company

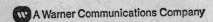

# DEDICATION

To Thomas J. O'Neill, for no other reason than being a good friend whether he likes me or not and having a sense of humor above and beyond the call of duty.

# ACKNOWLEDGMENTS

Anthony F. Slez, Jr., who gets really good ideas that I can screw up.

Larry Hama, a very nice dangerous man who wouldn't hurt a fly. Everything else, maybe, but not a fly.

Hansen & Co., Gunsmiths, who have everything I need to hurt flies.

Steven Hartov, who has good parents and a bad armory.

Jim Frost, who is very adaptable and gracious.

The Atlantic City Chamber of Commerce, who never answer their phone.

# Chapter One

She felt him slide into her as his hand went over her mouth and the gun barrel jammed against her ribs. She couldn't understand what was happening for a second. The gagging hand was no big surprise. She had serviced men who were into bigger bondage than that, but the gun was unexpected. First off, she hadn't noticed he was carrying it. She hadn't been in the business that long, but long enough to pride herself on spotting a piece. Second, the john hadn't said anything about a rape fantasy.

He continued to hump her on the creaking bed without a word, however, so Vicki Kelly allowed herself to relax and continued to ply her wares in the darkened room. She thought a rape fantasy isn't really valid without the element of surprise for some people. Rape, by its nature, was forced sex without acceptance, and what she was experiencing was anything but that. So Vicki made little noises under the heavy hand and struggled weakly against the sexual assault while she looked indifferently out of the room's one window.

The ocean was beautiful, as always. At night, even with the Boardwalk bustling with activity and the twinkling lights of the born-again ,Atlantic City making a multi-colored "connect-the-dots" pattern on the shore, the water always soothed her. She was sorry the john hadn't let her keep the window open. She loved the sea breezes rippling across her body during sex. It was usually a far more pleasant sensation than the sex itself. The act of copulation had stopped being a joy long ago. Ever since Eric had gone.

She felt her body automatically responding in the time tested way. The blood drifted from various areas of her body into the blood vessels inside her vagina. She got that slight light-headed feeling she always got and then it was all over. The john had spent himself. She felt his body slacken for a second, but the lukewarm metal of the gun barrel stayed tight against her side and the hand remained clamped over her lips.

"Don't make a sound," the john whispered, "or I'll blow your boobs off."

Inside Vicki smiled at the threat. The little boy was trying to talk dirty to her. The rape fantasy was continuing. Maybe he was going to move into her again. That would cost him extra. Outside, she kept her face innocently confused and frightened. She kept her eyes wide and gave a tiny nod. But inside, she was very glad that she worked at the Shop. If she had been an independent, the guy might've gotten into her room with a real gun. At best, he could've then left without paying. At worst, he could do what he threatened.

But there was no way Lenny would let a guy with a real weapon into her room. He must've been searched as he told them his fantasy and they supplied him with an empty pistol before sending him up. The Shop had spent a lot of time and a lot of money to get established. There was no way Lenny was going to let a card-carrying crazy loose among his girls. He worked with only a core of the best. He had too few and they were too good to risk damage.

Vicki, especially. She prided herself as one of the Shop's prime attractions. Not only did she have a rich mane of auburn hair, big dark eyes, and a sleek, full body that was the envy of the East's new Gold Coast, but she was versatile. She liked being whatever the john wanted her to be. The overdeveloped schoolgirl, the ravaged society woman, the kidnapped princess—whatever. She prided herself on her performances in her well-appointed room in the Shop, overlooking the Atlantic. It proved to her, at least, that she had the acting talent everyone else said she didn't.

She felt the steel leave her side. The john pulled himself out of her and shrugged up to sit on her stomach, his knees pinioning her arms to her sides. She looked up over his muffling hand to get her first real glimpse of his face. The rainbow of tiny colored lights from outside dimly illuminated his visage. At first it seemed wide, strong, and rugged. After a second, however, Vicki could see that the brown eyes were a little soft and a bit too close-set over the long nose. The high cheekbones ended in a tiny mound of loose flesh which would become jowls. And the wavy brown hair was forced into its casual position by the best hair styling money could buy.

One of the john's hands stayed clamped over her mouth while the other brought the gun up to point right between her eyes.

The silencer worried her. It was a big, thick, heavy thing with a tiny hole in it. It was not a rapist's gun. It was not a little empty snub-nose that Lenny would supply a john with. And the pressure he put on her arms and lips also concerned her. It was more than just enough to keep her meekly in place. Her muscles were beginning to ache in those areas. After a night full of sex, she didn't know whether she could actually break away from under him. She felt the confining terror of claustrophobia begin to wash over her. She twisted and bucked beneath him.

The john smiled as she struggled in vain. "That's nice," he said, his body moving but the gun staying steady. "That's real nice."

It was getting a bit frightening for Vicki. She wouldn't be able to get free, she realized. Then, with an effort, she calmed herself. It's all part of the game, she rationalized to herself. He had wanted her to struggle and she had struggled, that's all. She looked up over his hand into his face again. His expression seemed to agree with her. He looked to be experiencing a rush of power and command almost all her johns seemed to seek. He was in control; she was in his power. He had what he wanted, so Vicki would adapt.

"That's right," the john said quietly. "Just relax. There's nothing you can do. I know, trust me. I've been watching you for a while. I've gauged your strengths and your weaknesses. I know what you can do. And what you can't."

Vicki felt a sudden chill, as if the window had been thrown open. Something in his voice was tickling the edges of her mind. She had heard speeches like this one before. All her clients who were into discipline, and even some who weren't, had told her more or less the same thing at one time or another. They came to her in order to feel some sort of superiority over the female race without having to resort to violence. But there was something about the way this john said it which worried her all the more.

She couldn't tell whether he was really getting into the fantasy of it or whether he was serious. It was a very fine edge Vicki had to watch out for. If the john got too worked up, she might get bruised and tomorrow's appointments would have to be postponed. Lenny wouldn't like that. Vicki would like it even less.

"So just take it easy," the john went on, shifting his position atop her. "You have nothing to worry about. We're two of a kind, we are. I'm Irish too, y'know. Terry Flanaghan, that's my name."

Confusion assailed her again. What was going on? He had her pinned down. He kept her silent. He had a gun in her face and he was introducing himself. It wasn't a rape fantasy. She didn't know what it was, and that was really scary.

"As soon as I saw you, I knew I had to have you," he continued in a whisper. "I saw you out on the beach in that tiny crocheted bikini. I saw you walking in those shiny skin-tight pants and silk shirt with those high-heel shoes. I said to myself, 'what is this girl selling?' I said to myself, 'this girl is selling her ass all over the Boardwalk.' But I'll tell you, darling, T. Flanaghan doesn't pay for anything. You hear me? I don't pay for shit."

This guy was crazy, Vicki decided in shock. She had to rip her lips out from under his fingers and scream for Lenny. Lenny would wrap this guy in a knot and pull him apart like a party favor.

She twisted her head and tried to pry open her jaw. For a second his strong fingers kept her mouth closed like a vise, then she felt her upper and lower teeth unclamping slightly.

He felt it too. His hand slid off her mouth, but before she could make a sound, the same hand slammed down on her solar plexus. Her attempt to scream turned into a mere exhalation that got no farther than the closed door. Then the john's hand streaked down and came up with one of his own socks. As Vicki gasped for breath, he shoved it into her open mouth.

The gag sent her into paroxysms of hysteria. She

wrenched her body under him like a bull trying to throw its rider. He moved atop her like a practiced broncobuster, his knees still keeping her arms pinned and one hand still holding the sock in her mouth.

Vicki beat on his naked thighs with her fists and tried to call Lenny. She felt the man get heavier across her torso and the sock fabric tickling the back of her throat. She was beginning to choke. It only made her all the more desperate to escape. Her gag reflex began to work as she heard Flanaghan chuckle.

When she began to cough and gag, he hastily pulled the sock from her mouth. "Not yet," she thought she heard him say, as she instinctively sought air like a drowning woman. With a strength she never knew she had, Vicki clawed at his chest, successfully pulling herself out from beneath him.

Flanaghan's own panic helped. He didn't want her to die on him yet, so he had loosened up when she started choking. She pulled herself up toward the headboard of the brass bed while he pushed himself back.

Vicki swallowed a mouthful of air as she lunged over to the right, trying to stab a small, white button on the back side of the bedside table. At the same time, she formulated the name "Lenny" in her throat.

The bullet plowing into the night table just in front of her fingers stopped her motion and her shout. For a second, the room froze, then she jerked her head over to look at Flanaghan. The supposedly empty gun was pointed at her bare chest and the thick, heavy silencer was smoking. She hadn't even heard the cough of the automatic going off. The thick bedding and carpet must've muffled the fall of the ejected cartridge.

She looked from the gun to his face. It had an entirely different expression. It was one of almost glowing, delirious happiness. It was the look of a cunning wild animal with its helpless prey cornered.

14

The evil, insane visage seemed to rush at her like a flaming comet. She felt clawlike fingers wrap around the bottom of her face. She was hurled back, her head slamming against the brass tubing of the headboard and the thick plaster wall beyond that. Her vision was completely cut off by a sudden wash of orange and black, but she felt Flanaghan's body pin her upright torso against the pillows, the thick golden tubing, and the wall as well. The now-warm gun barrel was rammed up beneath her right breast.

In the moment after her head had been bashed up against the wall she saw and felt many things from her lifetime. She saw her mind's picture of Eric. It was the soft, homogenized vision of kind memory. She saw him as the thin, assured teen she had met in high school, and the casual musician she had lived with during college. She didn't remember his apathy, lack of responsibility, or indifference. She didn't see the man who had left her after she had become pregnant. She saw the man she first made love to. The man she felt sure had made love to her.

She saw their child. Not as it looked when it was born, but as it looked right now at the age of a year and a half. It was handsome, whole and aware. It reached out for life. It was a beautiful, affable girl who never cried. Her mother had done all the child's crying for her.

She saw her parents as if they were locked in an old-time sepia photo taken during the 1800s. They were expressionless, sedate, old-fashioned figures who renounced their daughter after her shame in the big city. They were a middle-class, Middle America couple who were more intent on living down their own shame than caring about their daughter's predicament.

She saw some of the faces of the men who couldn't help taking advantage of her. As well-intentioned as they were, they couldn't help her, and almost all of them wound up getting paid off with the only thing she had. She couldn't understand the truth: she was very attractive but not good-looking enough to make up for the fact that she had no talent. She was beautiful but she wasn't right for modeling. She was bright but she wasn't intelligent. Whatever pluses she had, she just didn't seem to have enough of them to get what she desired as fast as she wanted it.

She saw Lenny, who had taken one look at her after she failed to get a job at Atlantic City's new casinos and told her how to feed herself and the baby. He had taken her in right after the child's birth, before Vicki's figure had returned, paid the hospital bills, and prepared her to become the headliner of the prostitution crop. Six months later she had started and proved her worth. She had found a new family which was strong, professional, and considerate.

Slowly, Vicki came back to her room in the present. She saw the room's side wall dimly through a wash of her tears. She felt her naked body pressed between the bed and Flanaghan. She felt a big hand squeezing hard on her cheeks and jaw. And she heard the quiet, intense voice.

"You don't call for anybody," he instructed. "Nobody can hear you. Nobody's going to do nothing for you. The cops don't care, your bosses don't care, you don't even care. You're just a whore, right? You're just a fucking prostitute who'll sell her ass to anybody. You could've done better, but you didn't want to."

Vicki tried to speak, but the hand gripping her chin was too tight and too strong to make any coherent sound. And all the time, she felt the gun digging into her chest. Her eyes closed, the tears continued to stream from her eyes.

"Look, bitch," Flanaghan said. "You don't move a muscle, right? You don't say a word. You do anything and I'll be real happy to shoot you right in your damn tits." He was not used to saying so much and being in such command over women. The words seemed thick as they drooled out of his mouth, the end of each slurring into the one that followed it. "I'll blast you if you move. Don't move."

He pushed her face away and hauled himself off the bed. He started to move backward, keeping the gun aimed on her chest. Vicki watched him back up through tear-stained eyes. She glanced over toward the nightstand. She saw the tip of the white button peeking from the corner of the table. She looked back at the retreating man. By then, Flanaghan was just a silhouette near the door of the room. The only thing illuminated by the outside lights was the silencer of his gun.

Vicki looked at her legs. They were curled up against her hips on the bed. She became aware of her arms. When Flanaghan had thrown her back, they went up instinctively. Her fingers had wrapped around the top of the brass headboard and stayed there, frozen. She began to loosen her fingers now.

"Keep them up," a soft, deadly voice warned. Vicki grabbed the tubing again for dear life.

Maybe it was still just a fantasy, she prayed. Maybe he'd just go out the door, put the gun away and go downstairs like it had never happened. His clothes were on the chair by the door. Maybe he'd just get dressed and leave.

Vicki couldn't tell what was happening. Flanaghan had kept the room dark from the outset, which allowed him to bring the gun over without her seeing it in the first place. She heard his clothes rustling and her heart leaped with hope. But then she heard the same clothes fall to the floor. Flanaghan came back into the light carrying a brief-case.

"Please . . ." Vicki said almost with a sigh.

"I said shut up," Flanaghan exhaled violently. The words and delivery were brutal, but the sound wasn't loud enough to reach beyond the walls. "You had your chance," he said flatly.

Vicki still didn't understand. Chance for what? And

when? Flanaghan opened the case and started to move rhythmically around the bed.

"I watched you," he said, clicking one half of a handcuff around her right wrist. "I saw you wiggling your tail at everybody out there." He pulled her arm up and around the top most tube of the headboard. He had to pull hard to get her wrist, and then her arm, between the wall and the tubing. Then he clicked the other part around the tube itself. "Man, you had to bump it with a trumpet, didn't you, you little bitch." He repeated the same procedure with her other wrist.

Vicki was totally confused. She wore nice clothes, sure. She wore things she liked and that felt good. But she didn't wear anything other girls didn't wear. She looked up as Flanaghan clicked a third pair of cuffs around her wrists. Now she was attached to the headboard and her wrists were attached to each other. Flanaghan put the gun on the side table.

"Man, what a cow, I said to myself," Flanaghan went on. "Look at her, I said. The clingy leotards and the shorts and all that. God, what does she want from me?"

"I don't understand," Vicki wailed, looking up into his righteous face. "What do *you* want from *me*? Please, just tell me. I'll be happy to do whatever you want."

The words infuriated him. She had disobeyed his orders. His mouth opened to tell her to shut up again, but his mind sent his limbs to work before the words could come out. Blood infused his face, making it puff out and turn purple. He grabbed a handful of her hair and pulled up. Her eyes squeezed shut and her mouth opened wide to cry out but he shoved a red rubber ball into her mouth.

It was big enough to pry her teeth open and not fall down her throat. Then he started slapping hunks of thick tape across the bottom of her face.

She tried to spit the obstruction out, but the first piece

of tape blocked it. Then more and more of the sticky stuff was slapped into place from her chin to her nose and from one ear to the next. Vicki started screaming, but by then the noise was just a dim muffled bleat. She wrenched and pulled against the metal binding her to the bed. It groaned, creaked, and shook, but it wouldn't give. Desperate, she kicked out with her legs, which were still unrestrained. She hit the open briefcase, which slid off the mattress and fell to the floor. It hit with a thump and Vicki watched more rubber balls bounce across the floor, more reels of silver and black electricians' tape roll away and more handcuffs spill out.

Enraged, Flanaghan pulled her hair up and wrapped the tape around her head directly from the spool. He kept wrapping until the bottom of her face was completely masked. Then he let her hair down and moved around the bed to retrieve two more metal binders. Vicki watched him approach in numb horror. He grabbed her ankle and clicked one cuff in place. Then he pulled the piniomed leg to the side until half her leg was off the bed. Flanaghan clicked the other cuff around the frame beneath the box spring. He repeated this action on her other ankle.

Her hands were up, her mouth was sealed, and her legs were spread wide. Flanaghan retrieved his gun from the nightstand where he had left it after manacling her wrists and stood before her. They were both naked.

"What do I want from you?" he echoed sarcastically. "I don't want anything from you, bitch. You're not worth shit. You could've been a nice girl, but you had to be a whore, didn't you? That's all you're good for, isn't it? Just a hunk of meat for anybody to buy. For a price, you'll do it with anybody, won't you?"

Vicki tried to understand the incomprehensible, erratic rage that was driving him. He was a psychotic. A real rapist. A man whose inability to communicate led to a seething, murderous hate of everything. Try as she might, she couldn't understand it. All she knew was that she was helpless against him. She strained against the metal shackles that held her in place. She twisted and contorted, trying to shield herself from him. She pushed at the ball in her mouth with her tongue and pulled at the tape that held her lips around it, but she couldn't escape.

Suddenly she felt as filthy and shamed as he saw her. She was terrified of death, but at the same time wanted to die before he could do more horrendous things to her.

"Well," he said with a big smile. "I've paid enough. Let's see you do it with my piece." He brought the gun up, pointed it at the ceiling, and approached the bed.

As far as Vicki was concerned, she had already stopped living. In the enforced stillness and quiet of her bondage, she realized that she had died the moment Eric had left her. She had died again when her family refused to help. All her thoughts now were of her child. It was little Barbara who was really important. All that Vicki had loved was in that child. Vicki would be happy to give up her own life in place of her baby's. But the terrifying thing was that even if Flanaghan killed her, there would be no guarantee Barbara would live. This thought, this mental torture, made her determined to fight against the metal and plastic restraints even though it was impossible to escape.

Flanaghan ignored the writhings of the beautiful girl. He sat on the left side of the bed, looking down almost gently at her sweating, straining form. His expression was that of an obsessed scientist about to make his discovery after years of research. He centered all his concentration between her legs.

In these last moments, Vicki tried to make some sort of sense out of this insanity. She remembered that he had said her boss didn't care about her. Who? Lenny? Had Lenny been paid for Flanaghan to do this? And she remembered that he said that he was Irish, like her. But they didn't use last names here. Had he guessed because of her hair color? Was he told her name was Kelly? And if so, was he told about Barbara as well?

All these thoughts tended to make her ignore what Flanaghan was doing, but it wasn't enough to obliterate the sensation completely. He was pushing the barrel of his long, shiny automatic into her. She tried to pull away, but her back was right against the brass headboard. She tried to push him away, but the handcuffs held her arms above and behind her head. She tried to pull her legs together, but the other restraints held them apart. She felt the steel moving in deeper and deeper.

"That's right," Flanaghan said fervently. "There we are."

Vicki sobbed, the tears cascading down to gather along the lip of the electrical tape. Beside the man's cooing voice, her low, wracking sobs were the only sounds in the room.

The gun had penetrated her almost to the trigger guard. "Now for the finishing touch," he whispered. "The crowning touch . . ."

At that second, the door to the room flew open.

Vicki looked up and Flanaghan spun around as the door slammed against the opposite wall. Standing there was the silhouette of a man.

The girl nearly fainted with relief. It had to be Lenny or some other rescuer, she reasoned. Realizing that Flanaghan was more or less unarmed now, Vicki clamped down with all her muscles to keep the gun where it was. But to her surprise, he didn't even go for it. Instead he looked at the figure with a degree of surprise, then turned calmly back to her. She saw an expression the figure in the doorway didn't. It was one of immature shame.

"I told you to check the other rooms and bring whoever you found downstairs," said the man in the doorway, the light from the hallway flooding in around him.

"This is the only one," said Flanaghan. "I was . . . I was interrogating her about her boss."

"Naked?" the other man snorted. "Get your clothes on and do your job. Then get downstairs."

Flanaghan looked directly into the girl's eyes, his expression saying that somehow this was all her fault. He reached for his gun, grabbed it, and pulled slightly.

Vicki had yet to relax her muscles. Feeling her resistance, Flanaghan callously jerked the gun side to side and pulled the trigger twice.

The cough of the silencer was further muzzled by Vicki's flesh. She felt a horrible tearing inside. She heard a small splat as one bullet tore through her spinal column and out her back into the plaster wall. It was a merciful shot. All pain went with the shattered pieces of her backbone. She sighed behind the mound of tape as she felt death moving in.

The second bullet burrowed through her vagina into her stomach cavity. It plowed through muscle and flesh to embed itself among the organs in her chest. The coroner would later find it there.

She died as fecal matter poured out across the embedded gun.

"Shit" Flanaghan cursed, jumping back lest the stuff splash on him as well.

The other man couldn't help laughing. "It's what you deserve, asshole," he said. "Move your ass. I won't say it twice." Then he turned and went down the stairs, leaving the door open.

Flanaghan wrenched his gun out of the corpse, cursing all the while. The stench from the silenced automatic was awful and blood was streaked across the blue metal. The man wiped it on the bedding, then threw it to the floor as he retrieved his clothes. He only put on his shirt, pants, and shoes before he picked up the stinking gun, rolled up the rest of his outfit and quickly left the room. He closed the door behind him, already forgetting the beautiful woman inside and how much he had pervertedly wanted her.

The room was dark again, and empty, save for Vicki Kelly's corpse. She sat on the bed, still bound and gagged, her eyes peacefully closed, a pool of waste between her outstretched legs. It was a horrid way to go, with only the night to witness the cruel ignominy of it all.

The night . . . and one other.

The room stayed dark and breathless for a few minutes after Flanaghan left. The girl's corpse was silent and motionless. Then a breeze coursed across the bed. The sheets ruffled and her lifeless hair waved. Then, again stillness. A shadow moved across her face and then the pile of tape was pulled from her head. The hairs that invariably came with it couldn't hurt her. The shadows then centered around her hands. Seconds later, the chains fell away and the limbs floated down to her sides.

The shackles around her ankles were soon gone. Then she was lifted and placed gently upon the floor—away from her excretions. Then the shadows left her completely. A moment later the breeze washed across the room again. Finally all was still . . . and peaceful.

The whorehouse known as the Shop was empty. Empty of life, at any rate. Terry Flanaghan made his way down the hall from Vicki's room then trotted down the wide, red-carpeted steps along a painting-lined wall. He moved through the tastefully decorated lobby and back into the industrial-size kitchen. It was spic and span and empty as well, and it had the facilities to feed an army. But there would be no orgy of revelers tonight. The hit men had picked their time well.

Working on inside information, they waited until the last appointment of the evening on a night when only a skeleton staff and the house manager would be on duty.

Flanaghan went right to a door in the back of the pantry section and opened it to reveal another wooden stairway. He ambled down these new steps, savoring the sounds of terror that emanated from below.

He settled on the tile floor of the finished basement and turned from the staircase to see Lenny, the house mother, the cook, the butler, and four girls on their knees, their heads bent down and their hands cuffed behind them. In addition, their ankles were cuffed, their wrists and ankles attached by a third set of cuffs, and a rubber ball taped in each of their mouths.

Lenny, a big blond guy in a Hawaiian shirt, kept trying to raise his head, but a hit man directly behind him kept pushing it down. Besides Flanaghan, there were three other hitmen. Whoever was supplying the capital for this job wasn't taking chances, Flanaghan figured. At twenty-five-grand a man, someone was spending a cool hundred thousand dollars to put the Shop out of business.

"You ready, finally?" asked the man who had interrupted Flanaghan's playtime upstairs.

"Yeah," Flanaghan drawled, moving behind the bound, terrified figures. He had immediately noticed that each gunman was standing behind two of the victims. The interrupting hit man had Lenny and the house mother, the next man the cook and the butler, the third man two of the prostitutes. That left Flanaghan the last two whores.

He walked down the line, each victim twisting their heads to look at him as he passed. As he stopped, his two targets became extremely agitated. One looked ready to fall over.

"I told you," barked the head hit man. "You move and you die." The girl forcibly kept up on her knees, her head down, tears falling to the tile floor.

Flanaghan looked at his victims in the bright fluorescent lights of the cellar. They really had some numbers here, he mused. The last girl was a streaked blond in a long, slit, clingy dress. The other was a brunette in a silk shirt and designer jeans. Flanaghan looked over at the head man, as did the others. He looked away from Lenny for a second, then nodded.

At that moment, all the men shot the people kneeling before them. One shot each, quickly and cleanly into the backs of their heads with silenced automatics. As Flanaghan fired and fired again, he thought that was just what whore-bitches deserved. Die, whore-bitches, die. He watched in glee as the shiny floor was flecked with blood, flesh, and hair. Almost as one the eight people fell to the side. The only noise was the coughing of the weapons.

"All right," said the head man, nodding over a job that was almost completed. "Flanaghan!"

The Irishman looked over, surprised and angry for being singled out.

"Get the other girl down here," said the head man. "This is supposed to be a professional job."

"Aw, hell, the point is made," Flanaghan complained, waving his arm at the corpses. "Let's just leave her there."

"I don't ask twice," the head man said ominously. Flanaghan looked from face to face. All the others would back him up. Casually, the Irishman shrugged. "I think it's just wasted energy," he replied to save a little face, "but whatever you say." He turned heel and walked for the stairs.

"We'll wait a minute in the lobby," the head man warned.

Flanaghan stopped at the bottom step. He looked directly at his mission superior. "Whatever you say," he repeated, shrugging on his shoulder holster. As he went further up the stairs, he slipped on his jacket. He opened the basement door and went back through the kitchen, leaving the door open.

One of the other hit men looked to their leader. "Is he connected?" he wanted to know.

25

"Outside help," the boss man replied. "One of his first East Coast jobs." The boss considered the empty air for a minute. "One of his last, too, if he don't go by the rules."

"He seemed okay during the stakeouts," the third man muttered.

"Yeah, he watched real close because he was hot for the redhead," the leader answered with disgust. "Come on, let's get out of here."

They slipped their guns back into the pouches under their expertly tailored jackets and moved toward the cellar steps, the corpses ignored. They had done this sort of thing dozens of times before. Their victims had ceased being people to them. They were just dumb animals, like deer or elk or ducks or the hundreds of other things people got a kick out of killing.

The lead man moved up first, coming into the kitchen. Although the room was brightly lit with overhanging lamps, and the shiny silver metal of the pots, pans, cutlery, sink, stove, and tables reflected even greater illumination on the beige walls, he didn't see the small, lithe figure dressed all in black standing on the one-eighth-inch wide top frame of the cellar door.

The other two men didn't see the motionless living silhouette either as they emerged. But just as soon as all three moved completely into the room, the figure leaped.

Although that action sent him flying forward and up in the high-ceilinged kitchen, the athletic effort created absolutely no sound. Even as he was striking, the hit men didn't know what slammed into them.

His first prerogative was to keep the killing silent. He didn't want Flanaghan to be tipped off by anything. The second thing was to kill and extract the necessary information before Flanaghan reached the girl's room. Her new position would put him on guard.

His plan was put into action even before he hit the ground. Just as his toe came down to the level of the

26

second man's shoulder, he stretched the limb out and kicked back. He was dropping in between the second and third man so his kick hit the front of the second hit man's shoulder and spun him around to face the third.

Only he was now standing between the two. And before the second man could react and the third man walk into him he hit the second man in the throat with his iron-hard outstretched fingers, then let the equal and opposite reaction send his elbow back into the third man's throat.

The blow silenced both men perfectly. Following through with the one strike, he sent his horizontal arm into a vertical position, pulling his elbow out of the third man's neck, but sending his forearm smashing into the man's nose. He did it with such stunning force that the third hit man's nasal cartilage was driven up into his brain.

The black-garbed figure was motionless for one second as the second man gagged and the third man fell back down the cellar steps. He then jammed his hand forward again, slamming into the second man's jaw so the bone moved back and cut off the blood flow to his brain. The second hit man was immediately unconscious. It all happened within the space of a second.

The lead hit man turned as soon as he heard the noise behind him. But by that time his men were already falling and the man in black was punching out again. This blow struck a slightly different target on the lead man's neck. He felt the power of speech all but leave as well as most of his nerve endings. He felt paralyzed, rooted to the spot. All he could do was see, hear, and breathe.

He saw a dark figure in front of him. It looked like a human-shaped blind spot in the glaringly light kitchen. No part of this figure could be seen except for his eyes. These eyes seemed to burn into the hit man from the slit in the dark hood the figure wore. And then the sense of sight was taken from the hit man boss.

The figure's right hand took the form of a trident, his

thumb, forefingers, and middle finger becoming a trio of hooks. He swung this weapon up and then down, the longer fingers ramming right through the hit man's eyes and the thumb digging into one of his nostrils.

The three fingers dug into place like a clamp. The first two fingers were deep into the ruined eye sockets and the thumb firmly imbedded in the nasal passage up to the palm. The extreme pain was beyond comprehension, but the head hit man found he couldn't scream. He heard the horrible sound echoing through his skull but the kitchen itself remained absolutely silent. His mouth was wide open, but no words came out.

The two men stood completely still in the kitchen, the only movement being the blood which poured out the hit man's sockets and over the attacker's black-gloved hand. Then the hit man heard words which seemingly came from inside his own brain. He felt he could do nothing else but answer.

"Who sent you?" were the words. "Who paid you?"

Terry Flanaghan was not happy about going to see Vicki Kelly again. She was not the girl he thought she was. Not anymore certainly. She was just a whore, sure, but she had shit on him. That kind of thing did not fit his image of what a lady should be. Terry Flanaghan had always had a warped image of women. His mother had always humiliated him in front of his peers and all the girls seemed to laugh at him in school. His father worried about him, so before he was to go into the army, his dad had taken him to the local whorehouse to become a man.

He got a disease there, but his parents never knew about it. The army treated it and sent him to Vietnam where he learned a lot more about women. He saw some of them on R 'n' R and he even shot some others on a few patrols. You couldn't trust them. Those Saigon whores and the Vietnamese villagers were all the same. You couldn't trust them.

Back in the States, he found out where the real women were. They were on TV and in the magazines. Those girls were clean. They were perfect and always acted and looked beautiful. Of course, some acted like whores, but he didn't watch those shows more than once. And he ripped the pictures he didn't like out of the magazines.

When he couldn't find work anyplace else, Flanaghan looked into the market for murder. It was something the Government had taught him to do, and he didn't want his talent to go to waste. Besides, he was interested in it. He found out that there were many people interested in an expendable killer. To almost everyone's surprise who hired him, he survived every assignment without the cops being the wiser. His clients weren't sure whether that said something good about Flanaghan or something bad about the police.

Finally he had been tapped to be a fourth man in this operation. He had been assigned to the Shop stakeout to study the schedule, which was where he first caught a glimpse of Vicki Kelly and was lustfully smitten. As far as he could see, she was one of his dream women. Too good-looking to be real. But too real to be comprehended. She was both a whore and a dream girl to Flanaghan. He had to have her.

So he had her and then ripped her apart. She was just like all the rest. A dream girl was better as a dream, he decided as he reached the top of the stairs and turned toward her room. But as he did, he heard a sharp creak from behind him.

He spun and had his silenced automatic out before him. Over the barrel he saw a little door at the end of the hall swing slightly open. It was an unusual doorway in that its bottom was a few inches off the floor and it was smaller than normal. More like a rectangular portal than a door.

Curious, and slightly eager to get away from his cleaning responsibility, Flanaghan approached the opening.

It was situated on the right-hand wall at the other end of the hall from Vicki's room. It was in front of a little window. The hit man glanced out. Below him was a little yard and a fence. Beyond that was the Boardwalk, the beach, and the ocean. Even at the late hour, people dotted the Boardwalk, all laughing and happy as if all was right with the world. Flanaghan thought about shooting some of them down. Not seriously, but he knew it was within the realm of possibility that he would be sent to kill one of them one day, and that comforted him.

He returned his attention to the little door in the wall. With his gun barrel he swung it all the way open slowly. He could see some wooden stairs leading up into the darkness and then off to the right. Inside the door, he saw an old-fashioned light switch—the kind that twisted rather than flicked. He liked the touch. In fact he liked the whole house. It was Victorian in design and decoration. It fueled his fantasies. This stairway added more fuel to his imaginative fire. He pictured a secret attic room, filled with cowering whores.

Flanaghan smiled, brought his gun up, reached in and twisted the light into life. He heard the click and saw the illumination drop down from above. He could see the shellacked stairs clearly now, leading up to the right. He kept his gun at the ready and started up.

The room he rose into didn't disappoint him. It was small, but very atmospheric. The walls met a sharply sloping ceiling which made a pyramid. There were bay windows of different colors on each wall, sending shafts of different colored light across the wooden floor. There were yellow sections of light alternating with sections of shadow along the floor, the walls, and the ceiling. Along the room's sides were steamer trunks of all types, many covered with lacy beige linen.

And in the very center of the room, beneath the crown of the ceiling, amidst its very own pool of light and darkness, was a standing, old-fashioned baby crib.

Flanaghan carefully looked into every corner of the room to make sure no nursemaid or leftover prostitute would try to jump him or escape. Satisfied he was alone with the crib, he put his gun away and approached the little bed. Inside, nestled among blankets and pillows, a small child lay sleeping.

It was a beautiful baby, a wispy, satin tuft of blond hair on its head. Its face was quiet, innocent, and slightly smiling. It was an island of life, beauty, and hope in the death house the Shop had become.

Flanaghan felt a rush of power and perversion he had never felt before. He felt almost godlike. It was a moment where he knew he was truly a master of life and death. His own crushing ability seemed overwhelming to him now.

It was a whore baby, he told himself. Created by the miserable sex that was paid for. It was a horrible, loveless creation already warped and corrupted by its own genesis. It didn't deserve to live. It couldn't live.

Flanaghan reached inside his jacket and pulled out a long, wicked switchblade. He held it beside his grinning face and clicked it open. The blade gleamed even in the dim light of the attic nursery. It was the dull, deadly gleam of a razor-sharp blade which had been cleaned with dirt and blood many times. The hit man shifted it in his hands so that he held it in a plunging position, the hilt in his fist and the blade protruding from the bottom of the balled hand.

He looked at the sleeping baby, trying to fully realize that he was cutting off its life. He wanted to fully comprehend and accept this new strength. He thought about waking the baby first, but he didn't want any squeal to alert the other hit men downstairs.

Slowly, ceremoniously, Flanaghan held the blade over the center of the baby's body. He counted silently to himself; one, two, three. Then he pushed down with a sudden, sweeping viciousness.

The blade didn't move.

A sudden rush of light-headedness clouded Flanaghan's vision for a second. For a moment he wasn't sure whether he had actually pressed down or whether he had simply thought about pressing down. This time without counting the hit man stabbed downwards with jabbing strength.

Nothing happened. The knife, and Flanaghan's hand, stayed exactly where they were—floating in midair.

Flanaghan pulled his arm back. It came away from over the crib without problem. Its sudden movement was so surprising that Flanaghan stumbled back in a reflex action. He looked at his hand and the knife clutched within the fingers like it was some alien thing on the end of his arm. Then he looked back at the crib. There seemed to be nothing unusual about it. There were no electric eyes attached to it which would create a force field. There were no like devices on any of the walls.

Just to make sure, Flanaghan checked the room again. He returned to the crib in puzzlement. Then he got mad. He figured it had to be his own subconscious that was preventing him from killing the child. The kid had done nothing wrong, it wasn't its fault it had been born, so Flanaghan didn't have a psychological reason for killing it. But it was a whore child, he mentally yelled at himself. A bitch whore baby. It would not live through the night. No fucking bitch baby would stop him from killing.

Enraged, Flanaghan jabbed down at the child. His hand made it to the same empty space. The hit man pulled back in fear this time. Somehow he had hit empty air. He had felt it this time. He had hit the empty air as if it had been a Plexiglas shield.

The hit man reached down with his other hand very

slowly. He paused when he reached the blocked area. There was nothing there. His hand kept going. He couldn't bring himself to touch the baby, however.

The anger built up inside him again. This baby wasn't going to stop him from being the murderer he was supposed to be. It wasn't just a thrill kill anymore. It was a challenge to his very existence. In a frenzy, Flanaghan grabbed the knife in both hands, raised it above his head, and brought it down with all his might.

It should have gone completely through the child. It should have buried itself in the baby's chest and nailed the little girl to the bedding. It should have, but instead the blade tip stopped dead in midair a mere whisper from the baby's top blanket. Flanaghan nearly fell into the crib from the force of his blow and its sudden stop.

He pulled back, only this time, his arms wouldn't respond. Practically snarling like a badger caught in a steel-jaw trap, Flanaghan tried to wrench his hands away from the crib, but they would not budge. The hit man was sure he was going insane. That, or the LSD he had taken in Vietnam had come back to do a trick on his mind.

He looked wildly around the room for some sort of escape. Suddenly he became aware of a strange shadow directly in front of him. His jerking movements stopped as his brain struggled to make sense of what seemed an optical illusion before him. As far as he could tell, he was staring at a shadow on the wall. Only this shadow seemed three dimensional. And his own hands had become part of the shadow. He seemed to have reached into the 3-D shadow itself, like Alice's hands going through the looking glass.

He moved forward until he was standing right against the crib and was not ten inches from the edge of the shadow. On closer inspection, he saw that it was all just a cunning camouflage. Someone dressed all in black had positioned himself so perfectly that all his limbs blended in with the shadows behind him. His body was contorted in such a way that not an inch was in the dim yellow light.

Then Flanaghan suddenly realized what he was seeing and he gave a small start. Immediately two steel-gray eyes opened in the darkness directly in front of him. The pressure on the hit man's hands was not released as the figure in black swung his leg up over the crib in a vicious arc. Only when the full side of the black-covered foot slashed across Flanaghan's jaw, were his hands released. Then the Irishman flew to his right to collide forcefully with the attic wall.

Flanaghan staggered, but he did not fall. His eyes were tearing and his vision blurred, but he did not lose consciousness. When he could see clearly again, he realized he still had the switchblade out before him, gripped in both hands. He looked up from it to see the figure in black—just barely discernible in the pale, low-watt light—still directly in front of him.

The only solid material things about this man were the eyes—eyes that seemed to hover in space. They were calm, full eyes. Eyes that seemed to possess some secret knowledge at the same time that they promised peace—a permanent peace.

Flanagahan's mind told his hands to bring the blade up and bury it between those gray eyes. But before his arms could respond, the figure was in a blurring motion. As if they were in a comic, albeit sadistic, "Three Stooges" movie, the black-garbed figure slammed his own fist down on Flanaghan's two clenched fists, sending the knife blade arcing right into the hit man's own crotch.

The blade cut through the pants, penetrated his penis, and sliced into his testicles.

The pain paralyzed the hit man for a second. Even in Vietnam, he didn't believe such excruciating pain could exist. It was a burning electric pain which seemed as if all his nerve endings had been dipped in acid.

Flanaghan finally managed to pull the blade out of his private parts, but it was a blind, automatic movement. His eyes were squeezed shut from the pain and the removal of the knife didn't put an end to the excruciating pain. The only thing that brought Flanaghan's attention back to reality were the words he heard.

He heard his own words, whispered in the room by another voice. A bland but strong, almost hypnotizing voice that sent the words directly into his mind—where they remained forever.

"Now for the finishing touch," said the voice. "The crowning touch . . ."

Flanaghan opened his eyes in time to see the figure kick out with the speed which made his leg a blur. The toes behind the black stockings acted like an ax which cut away the remaining rended flesh covering his pelvis. The kick ripped off his balls and most of his penis. He felt the devastating foot go further through his body until it finally rested in his intestines. The foot held him upright.

Then the black-suited figure pulled his foot out and punched Flanaghan in the throat. The hit man's guts started pouring out of the hole between his legs. He tried to scream but his vocal cords seemed crushed. He fell to the attic floor, his eyes wide open but unseeing, his mouth opening and closing soundlessly, and his hands still wrapped around the bloody switchblade.

The man in black stood watching until Flanaghan lay perfectly still with his eyes glazed over. Only then did the hit man's assassin reach up and pull his hood back. The face that was exposed was a calm, innocuous one with short sandy hair. It was the face of Brett Wallace.

The only American Ninja Master turned away from the corpse and looked to the child in the crib. It was still sleeping. Brett had seen to it that the noise of his killing would not disturb it. It was only the stench of death now in the room that might have woken it up. Thankfully, it did not. Brett looked at the sleeping little girl and let his mind drift.

Brett looked away from the baby and out the attic window. The sea sparkled with the reflected lights of the shore. Brett felt the same false peace Vicki had felt when looking at the serene ocean. He didn't blame himself, nor did he feel pity or shame, but he was sorry he couldn't have saved the girl. He had been following the hit men and while she was being murdered, he was looking for a way in.

There were no windows in the cellar so he couldn't rescue the other prostitutes either. By the time he had climbed the outside wall to her window, she was already dead. By the time he had climbed in and reached the kitchen without being seen or heard, the basement massacre was over as well. All he could do then was avenge their deaths and save the child.

Now he had to cover his tracks. He had found the sawed-off shotgun Lenny kept on the premises but couldn't get to it when the hit men had attacked. He would use that on the faces of the head hit man and the one he sent down the steps to cover the fact that he had mashed their faces. Then he would shoot the unconscious hit man with the other men's guns. Next, he would uncuff Lenny and put the shotgun in his hands. With the right positioning, it would look as if Lenny used the second hit man as a shield while killing the first and third assassins. Before they died, they shot the second man trying to get to Lenny.

Finally Brett would make Flanaghan disappear. Then all the police could do was suppose the fourth hit man had killed Lenny and got away. The cops would also find no traces of the child. Brett had other ideas for her instead of the casual, unconscious cruelty of life in state homes and orphanages.

Looking out at the dark, deep sea, Brett was suddenly

assailed by the overwhelming sense of loss he occasionally felt. He hadn't felt many true emotions since the death of his wife and family, but he did feel loss, a bottomless chasm where the injustices of the world could be dropped. He was as yet unsure what brought death to this place, what murdered the other prostitutes and the mother of this child, but he was going to find out and repay the executioner in kind.

Brett turned back into the room and went to work. The innocent baby slept through it all, oblivious.

# Chapter Two

Two weeks before the Shop's massacre, an elderly man took a motorcycle chain blow right across the chest.

The poor guy was too old to even cry out in abject pain. His wrinkled mouth simply opened, his gray-topped, thick-veined head went back and he fell into the arms of the elderly citizens behind him.

The blow came out of nowhere for no reason. He was simply walking in the company of six other senior citizens when a young punk told him to "Hold it." When he stopped, the teenaged offender pulled the chain from behind his back and let the old man have it.

"All right," said the punk, who was wearing a baseball jacket over a T-shirt and jeans on the balmy September day in San Francisco. "Let that be a lesson to you old geezers. Nobody calls the cops on the Crimson Knights and gets away with it." As he spoke, four other kids appeared from the mouth of an alley to the right of the sidewalk. Each carried a different implement. One had an ax handle, another a baseball bat, the third a sock full of pennies, and the fourth a club with a protruding nail.

"You can't do this!" the old man who was hit gasped. "You take our checks, you terrorize us, and then you beat us if we try to stop you. You can't get away with this."

They were facing each other on a narrow, sloping street across the way from an empty, garbage-strewn lot with a chain-link fence around it. The buildings in every direction were rundown brownstones almost totally occupied by retirees without protection. The confrontations between these elderly residents and the street gangs were common occurrences. As the face-off started, windows began to close everywhere on the block.

"You hear?" said the old man. "You hear? One of those people will call the police. They'll see for themselves now."

The kid with the motorcycle chain laughed. "That's what you think," he said, and spat. "You're crazy, old man. Those folks are hiding under their beds. We know every one of them and they know there's no door or lock that will keep us out."

"And even if somebody calls the cops," piped in the one with the bat, "they don't care about you. You got no money, you got no clout. Now us, we got rich parents! We're in the upper middle class!" The rest of the young hoods laughed at the sarcastic description.

"Besides," said the holder of the cycle chain, "even if the cops do come, it'll be over long before that. We're young and we can fight. Who's going to fight for you, old man?" The chain holder motioned to the others. All five started to move in.

The group of oldsters cowered on the sidewalk in front of them. Behind the first old man was a thin old lady who was quaking with fear and a chubbier old woman whose expression showed cowed resignation. Behind her was a terrified fat man using a cane to walk. The third old man was small and bald. The last old man was kneeling behind the fallen man. His face was masked by a thick mustache and beard that covered the bottom of his face. His eyes were masked by a battered slouch hat atop his head. The contours of his body were camouflaged by a worn, baggy suit.

The first hoodlum stood over the elderly group for a second, then swung the chain at the fallen man with savage speed.

The rest of the old people gasped in horror as the thick metal seemed destined to bury itself in the first man's skull. The links whistled through the air, but at the last possible second, they wrapped around a wrist that was thrust between the teenager and his target.

The ching-ching-ching of the links clacking against each other as they wrapped around the wrist ended with a clittering clank as the loose end of the chain slapped into the palm attached to the wrist, the fingers closed on the end and the entire interrupting arm pulled.

The first punk snapped forward, then was hurled back when his chin collided with the heel of an empty hand thrust forward as the chain hand was swiped back. The sound of the kid's jaw against the bony heel of the open hand was a significant smack.

The kid flew back three feet, completely off the ground, his head bent back as far as it would go without breaking his neck. He landed on the sidewalk flat on his back, his head cracking against the concrete with another nasty sound that was crunchy and splashy.

Everyone was shocked into stillness for a second. The new tableau had four kids staring at their fallen spokesman as the elderly group looked up at the bearded man who was standing amidst them, one hand back—filled with the cycle chain—and the other hand forward, the fingers bent clawlike.

The teen quartet looked to the bearded old man. "I'll fight for them," the man said in a bland, even tone.

As if psychically cued, the other gang members charged him, each screaming and brandishing their individual weapons. The bearded man's hands lashed out in two directions at the same time. With his left hand he brought the chain around to go coursing right through the sock full of pennies and then into the face of the kid that held it. He swung the chain with such force that the released coins spread out with the speed of buckshot. The kid's face was torn open by the copper disks and the metal links of the chain.

The youth holding the bat swung it at the man's head, and the man threw up the edge of his hand to meet it. The result was as if the kid were trying to knock aside a falling redwood tree. He watched in amazement as the bat cracked and then broke in two from the force of the blow to the man's hand. The top half of the bat soared harmlessly over the bearded man's head and bounced down the sidewalk.

The bearded man did not remain still. Seemingly with the speed of lightning, he pivoted to send the side of one foot into the approaching kid with the ax handle. The man grabbed the ax handle in both hands as his foot sunk into the young hood's solar plexus. The feet went forward off the sidewalk as he bent double. It was like running into an iron tube. He fell on his buttocks, his internal organs mashed and several ribs broken.

The bearded man altered his stance again, the ax handle in his hands. He swung it to catch the tip of the club that the last kid was swinging. With his superior force, the man deflected the club to slam into the side of the kid with the broken baseball bat. The nail protruding from the club did most of the damage. The bat bearer fell to the street, the club still attached to his side. The final boy was left standing, unarmed and amazed.

The bearded man dropped the ax handle and straightened. The first kid was still unconscious. The second kid was clutching at his gashed face and screaming. The third was pulling the nailed club out of his side, crying through clenched teeth. The fourth kid fell back with a groan, clutching his stomach. The last kid stared at the bearded man, his mouth wide open.

He started backing up slowly, his hands out at his sides. Then he trotted backwards until he almost fell off the curb. Finally he spun around and ran into the street toward the empty lot, nearly getting hit by a hastily braking car.

The bearded man turned to the astonished group of senior citizens with a smile. He reached into his pocket and pulled out a roll of money, which he pressed into the hands of the fatter woman. "See to his injuries," he instructed them, nodding toward the old man who had been chain-whipped. "Let their rich parents see to their children. I don't think they'll bother you again."

Then he turned and jumped at the same time. The old people watched an incredible leap which took the bearded man to the roof of a parked car then over to the roof of the braked car then onto the opposite sidewalk. The final kid was desperately climbing the high chain-link fence around the lot. He had almost made it to the top when the bearded man landed on the wide sidewalk, somersaulted, then leaped up again to fly over the climbing kid, grab onto the top of the fence and hold onto the opposite side, waiting for him.

Before the kid realized what had happened, he placed his fingers on the top links. He looked up to see the bearded man's smiling face. Before he could let go, the bearded man's fingers wrapped around his from the other side. The kid let his feet go slack, but the bearded man was holding him up with just his fingers.

"You visit your friends in the hospital," the man instructed the kid in a low voice. "And you tell them. The next time they hurt anybody else but themselves, it's death. It can come from anywhere and from anybody. And the next time they touch any money that isn't their own, this will happen."

The bearded man squeezed. The last kid felt the pain, then he heard the popping and cracking of his finger joints and bones. He saw his skin start tearing and streams of blood come coursing out. They flowed down the back of his hand and dripped onto his contorted, sweating face.

"For your crimson nights," said the bearded man, and then he let go. The kid fell back to the sidewalk. The bearded man dropped down to the empty lot and ran off in the opposite direction. It wasn't until he vaulted over the opposite fence with one leap and ran five more blocks that he found a crowded bar, went into the restroom and started peeling off his disguise.

His hat had stayed on because it was part of the wig. Pulling it off revealed his crop of sandy short hair. The beard and mustache came next, revealing the fairly young face of a man in his mid-thirties. Than the real magic began. The man's complete carriage changed. His posture altered, his shoulders went back, the curvature of his spine straightened and wrinkles on his forehead and cheeks all but disappeared by the relaxing of muscles he had tightened across his visage.

Underneath the long, baggy jacket was a light blue button-down cotton shirt which he had filled out upon straightening up. The pants weren't that bad. The waist fit, so they simply looked like the new fashions which billowed out from the belt. Brett Wallace looked at his placid reflection in the mirror, put the wig, hat and beard into the coat, folded the coat over his arm and left the lavatory.

"Mister," he heard in his ear among all the other bar sounds. He attributed it to a stranger calling a friend nearby. He had spent so much time as a professional non-entity he almost felt as if he was actually invisible. Allowing the word to be swallowed up by the bar's smoky interior, Brett pushed himself toward the exit door.

"Mister," the voice came again. Brett instinctively categorized it. It came from a man, about five feet, ten inches tall, and at least seventy-five years of age. Brett turned and looked into the face of an age-spotted gentleman in a yellow shirt and multicolored double knit slacks. Even that tightly woven material was baggy on the painfully thin fellow, kept up by a worn leather belt.

"Please, mister," the man said, as if he were a frightened child talking to a private eye. "You're the one who helped us, aren't you?"

The elderly man said the last two words as if he had been pushed to ask. Brett could have easily said "no" and made the answer stick. He knew the method with which to ensure absolute belief. The man would have walked away positive that Brett was not the man he sought. But something about the fellow's sad eyes and unsure approach kept Brett from rebuffing him. No man who reached that age should be that humble or insecure.

Brett nodded in response. "Yes," he said softly.

"Please," the man repeated, taking Brett by the arm. "Please come with me for a moment. It's very important."

Brett let the old man lead him past the crowded bar and into the rear of the watering hole, lined on both sides with wooden booths and round tables. They stopped by the farthest booth on the left, where a small, round old woman sat. Her pocketbook was on her lap and she had both hands clutching it. Brett recognized her as one of the old people he had defended.

44

She looked up at him as if looking into the eyes of a stranger, but only at first. Her eyes wavered away from his warm gaze for a second and then a satisfied smile drifted across her face. "It's you," she said. "You are the one."

Brett motioned for the man to sit down. He slid in next to the woman. Brett took up a sitting position across the table from them. He kept his expression sympathetic but curious. Inside, he was amazed the woman knew who he was. "How did you find me?" he asked.

"People don't notice things they see every day," the old woman said, still smiling. "And they don't like to be reminded of their own mortality. So an old person walking down the street is ignored. There are millions of us, but the only ones who notice are the muggers."

"Diane," said the old man, "please. You are rambling." Brett smiled at her name. Actually he smiled at himself. For he had thought "Diane" was an unusual name for an old woman. For some reason, he thought every old woman was named Bertha, or Agnes, or Gladys, or Agatha. Names like Mary, or Jennifer, or Diane seemed the sole property of teenagers. Brett eliminated that conceit from his mind and listened to what the old man had to say.

"We followed you. We searched the blocks—all of us— until I caught a glimpse of you coming in here. When you went into the lav, I called Diane on the phone. She came right down. And when you came out looking different, she was sure it was you. I don't know how."

Brett laughed. "Neither do I. Well, Diane, what can I do for you? Why were you so anxious to catch up with me?"

The woman opened her pocketbook and took out a soiled photo. She placed it on the table and slid it across to Brett. The younger man could see it was a Polaroid print of an extremely attractive young woman. She

45

was dressed in a shirt and shorts, laughing at a backyard barbecue.

"My daughter," the woman said. "Victoria. Vicki."

Brett examined the wrinkled, bent photograph. He could tell the auburn-haired beauty was very young, but gave the impression of maturity. She was the kind of girl her high school peers would label "haughty" simply because she seemed more of a woman, although it was just as likely that she would struggle through a life of indifference and envy simply because no one would give her a chance. In a way, she was too good-looking for her own good.

"I haven't seen her for years," Diane went on. "She became pregnant and . . . well, her father and I . . . misunderstood. We . . . it was our fault she . . . I tried to . . ." The woman choked off the words.

"It has been very bad," the old man took up, allowing Diane to look away and dab at her eyes with a hanky. "They couldn't bring themselves to forgive the girl. They felt they drove her out. And there is not very much an unmarried woman can do with a child. Except . . . except . . ."

Now it was the old man's turn to drift off. He couldn't bring himself to say it anymore than the woman could.

"It's all right," said Brett. "I think I understand. Except where do I fit in with all this? Is she in any kind of trouble?"

"She's in Atlantic City," the old woman told him, pulling herself back together. "New Jersey," she added just in case he didn't know. "She has been sending me money every week since her father died. She never includes any letter, but I know it's from her. And the postmark says Atlantic City."

"So?" Brett couldn't help but ask.

"She *had* not sent any letters," the old man explained. "In the last envelope she did. It said . . ."

"It said," Diane interrupted, "that she was happy and doing well, but things had gotten strange where she worked. She said she needed someplace to go for a little while . . . until 'things cooled down a bit,' she said. That was two weeks ago. I haven't heard from her since. I've been worried sick. I was just coming back from the post office when those young hoodlums stopped us."

"And you stepped in," said the man.

The woman dug into her purse again. "This was in the mail," she said, holding up an envelope. "It's the same amount of money, but it is a check, and it is not signed by her."

Brett took the paper. He translated the scrawl on the bottom right as "Lenny Hansen."

"You know all the terrible things that go on in Atlantic City," Diane said. "All the judges and police on the take, everybody knows that."

"Diane, please," the old man interrupted, embarrassed. "Please, mister. I wouldn't have bothered you, but Diane, she's been so afraid."

"Could you find my daughter?" the old woman asked. "I know it is a lot to ask, but there was no one else I could go to. I'll pay you. I'll give you everything I have. I just want to make up for what my husband did—what my husband and I did to her."

Brett listened, the smile fading from his face. He put the girl's good looks, her need for money, her sudden wealth, and the man's name together. It all spelled "prostitution." And the hooker game in Atlantic City was not your run-of-the-mill "wham, bam, thank you ma'am." He was honestly touched by the old woman's plight.

She was confused, unsure, practically helpless. The cops wouldn't help. Her daughter was not really a "missing person." Even with her daughter's contributions, she probably didn't have enough to sustain a private investigator for very long. She was gripped in an unidentified fear. She had a mother's sixth sense for her daughter's safety and Brett could see it was driving her crazy.

He took her frail, shaking hands in his. "No money will be necessary," he said. "I'll see what I can do." The woman's face lit up with a beacon of renewed hope and thankfulness. "But on one condition," Brett added. Her face lost its joy, to be replaced by doubt.

"What is it?" she asked with trepidation.

"You tell me how you knew I was the one who defended you."

The old woman laughed. "When you get to my age, you see things many others miss. You can change your clothes, you can grow or cut off hair, you can wear lifts on your shoes, you can use contact lenses, you can even get plastic surgery. But the one thing you forget to change are your ears. You can't change your ears. Each one is as individual as a fingerprint. Remember that, young man."

It was late afternoon when he got back out onto the San Francisco streets. He had been dogging the elderly group's trail since early morning. He knew that their Social Security checks were coming that afternoon, so he assumed the Crimson Knights would be waiting somewhere between the mailboxes and the bank to steal the money and punish the old man for complaining to the cops.

Brett knew what was going down because he read the complaint report on microfilm right out of the police files. And he read the newspapers and city magazines which occasionally touched on the battles between senior citizens and the street gangs. And he listened in on CB, ham, and police radio conversations.

Once he got the setup straight, it was then only a matter of adapting a suitable disguise and blending in with the group so that the gang and the elderly folk themselves hardly knew it. The Crimson Knights were looking directly at him during the whole confrontation, but he saw to it that they didn't realize he was new or different.

Brett reached the corner of Market Street and Van Ness Avenue, and looked at the architectural magnificence of the Civic Center. He took in the domed City Hall, the classically handsome opera house, and the old main library as he thought about the art which enabled him to blend in and kill.

The Crimson Knights had been defeated by three basic things even before Brett had started fighting. *Chikairi-no-jutsu,* the art of infiltration which allowed him to blend in with the senior citizens without anyone noticing; *Kuji-kiri,* the art of distraction, which had the hoods concentrating on one thing insead of another; and *Saiminjutsu,* the wonderfully effective art of suggestion and imagination. All three blended to defeat the gang of hoodlums even before the first blow. They were but three of dozens of ancient arts taught Brett by the Oriental masters of ninjutsu: the art of stealth.

Brett checked the San Francisco autumn sky and his own internal clock. It was after seven-thirty and his dojo's last class would be in session. Brett changed his course and headed in the direction of the martial arts school that he had created. He found himself in front of the Dawn Dojo just before nine o'clock.

Utilizing his talents, he entered unseen and stood in the studio doorway as Jeff Archer finished his last class of the day. And although Brett stood in the doorway for eight minutes—in full view of Jeff and reflected in the wall-length mirror in front of the students—not one person noticed him.

For months Jeff had asked him how such a thing was possible. There were times when Brett could make himself invisible. At one point, Jeff had been witness to a situation where a man had looked directly at Brett from a distance of three feet and had not seen him.

"It is not simple," Brett had finally replied, "but the science of it can be introduced simply. In a way, it is a capsule description of the entire ninjutsu art.

"Have you ever dropped a pen while writing something and looked down to where you think it landed, only it isn't there? And have you searched for that same pen for many minutes in vain? Finally, in frustration, you get another pen only to look down and see the pen right in front of you. Through mental tricks of anticipation, imagination, and suggestion, the pen was all but invisible to you. Essentially, I make myself that pen. Through all my art, I place myself where you are sure I can't be. Therefore, to you, I'm not."

As difficult as it was to explain, it was hundreds of times more difficult to master. Since returning from the Orient and his own advanced training, Brett had been seriously instructing Jeff in a higher plane of martial arts so that the young man could be *genin*—an agent—to Brett's *jonin* or master.

So Brett now watched the five-foot, nine-inch Archer with the brown hair and tough triangular face, teaching the rudiments of karate to his seven-thirty to nine o'clock class.

"The final, and most important thing to remember about karate," Archer was intoning, "or judo or akido or any of the martial arts, is that to do it properly it must be considered more than a way to break blocks of ice with your head." The class tittered and chuckled at this. "It is a way of life," Archer continued. "It is an acknowledgment that we are more than skin, muscle, bone, and blood. That there is a power inside that we can only harness with a full awareness. And this awareness means more than just the practiced physical technique. It means a rich mind, a rich soul.

"The mind is the key, the controller of the body. If it is sick, if there is an illness there, you cannot hope to master anything. You will be doomed to failure in everything you do." He paused to let the information sink in. "Now, get on out of here, it's been a hard day."

The class slowly broke up for the night. They took their texts on Oriental history and art, which Archer insisted they study in addition to other courses, and left in groups of two to six. Each of the class members had found they had something in common. Archer always felt good about that. The way he taught weeded out those interested in simply breaking bricks with their teeth.

Only when everyone else had left did Brett speak up. "Now it's your turn for lessons, teacher."

Jeff leaped around in shocked surprise. When he saw Brett, he leaned against the mirrored wall while clutching his heart in mock shock. "How do you *do* that?" he wailed with humor.

"You'll find out," Brett answered, looking at his wrist as if there was a watch there, "in about ten years."

Jeff picked a towel off a wooden folding chair and mopped his sweating brow with it. He was dressed in a black, U-neck, sleeveless T-shirt and kung-fu pants tied at the waist. He was barefoot. "How did it go today?"

"A lot easier than last time," Brett said with relief, remembering how he and Jeff met.

"I hope so," Jeff replied, putting the towel down, and looking back at Brett with concern. "It never stops, does it?"

Brett didn't answer. He just walked from the door across the room.

"I mean," Jeff elaborated. "If it isn't the gang that killed my grandmother, it's the Crimson Knights. And after them, it'll be another gang. As long as their are old people and bored creeps . . ." Jeff let his curse trail off as Brett stopped in front of him.

The older man shrugged. "That's what we're here for. Let's do a little limbering up tonight."

Brett's idea of "a little limbering up" would break the back of almost anyone else. The two men went from the main studio to a locked and bolted door leading to a cavernous subterranean room lined with special martial arts paraphernalia, in addition to a fully equipped lab. When it was first built and outfitted to Brett's specifications upon his return from Japan, Jeff considered it the Ninja Master's "Batcave," alluding to the secret headquarters of the fictional superhero Batman.

Brett had to agree with Archer's estimation, but what served Batman so well in fantasy did the same for Brett in reality. In this quiet place, Brett practiced with all the classic ninja weapons: the swords, the bow and arrow, the dirks and knives, the *bisento* or spear, the *toniki* or throwing spikes, the *shaken* or *shuriken*—multiple-pointed throwing stars, the *kusari-gama*—a three-foot chain with a weight on one end and a hatchet on the other, and the *kyotetsu-shoge*—an elastic cord with a weight on one end and a two-edged blade on the other.

Brett worked with each of these until he became so skilled that he could shave a man's five-o'clock shadow with any one of them. But recently he was working more diligently on perfecting the art of making the commonplace deadly. It was increasingly more difficult for Brett to pack his ninja weapons on his missions of vengeance. It was only on the rare trip when he was able to deck himself out in the entire lightly armored arsenal to lay waste to an army. He had done it on the "Mountain of Fear" in Virginia, but not since then. The correctable evil he was finding was in the major urban centers, where the law enforcers frowned on decapitated suspects and a pile of dismembered villains.

So Brett worked on his killing skill with everyday items. Pens, pencils, newspapers, straws, coins, ice cubes, light bulbs, needles, darts, tacks, scissors, screwdrivers, forks, spoons, brooms, ashtrays and most available things, including the most deadly weapons of all: his hands and feet. Brett worked strenuously to make them the fastest and most precise killing implements possible.

Tonight Jeff set up a row of sixteen candles and a six-pack of capped full beer bottles while Brett meditated. Then the Ninja Master rose and approached the first eight candles. They were tall and thick, making his job all the more difficult. Without making a sound, Brett sent his right hand across in a blinding arc, just barely touching the tip of each flame but creating enough suction to blow all eight candles out.

Without a word, he stepped over to the next eight. Nonchalantly he made a fist at the level of his waist. Then by pivoting sideways while punching out and pulling the fist back almost all at the same time, he put out the remaining eight candles one at a time. It wasn't the initial punch that did it, it was the speed at which he pulled the fist back. That created the vacuum which snuffed out the flame. Brett did it quickly and silently.

"Light them again and place them four and a half feet from the wall," Brett instructed. While Jeff was doing that, Brett approached the beer bottles which were placed on a table two feet from each other. There were three on one edge of the table and three on the other. He stood quietly in front of the first bottle for a second. Then his palm edge lashed to the side so fast it seemed to jump from his right side to his left side magically. A short rending screech filled the room for a second. Archer looked up from the candles to see the beer bottle cut in half. Not shattered, not broken, but sliced, sheared in two pieces by Brett's blinding blow.

Archer was about to express his admiration at the feat when he realized that Brett was still deep within the concentration necessary to do such an amazing thing. This concentration was integrated into him enough, however, that Brett was not reluctant to speak.

"I've seen Shihan Torii open a capped bottle without a strike," Wallace said, moving in front of the second bottle. With a second swipe of his right hand, he cut that in half as well. The top part, with the liquid, spilled onto the table, rolled across, and fell to the floor. "He just grabbed the bottle in both hands," Brett continued, going on to the third bottle, "and held it."

Brett hacked at the third bottle with his left hand. The bottle separated, its edges smooth and flat. "At first it looked as if he wasn't expending any effort at all," Brett went on, moving around the table to the fourth bottle, "but I could see how powerful his concentration was." His left hand shot out again, cutting the fourth bottle in two.

"A few seconds later the cap just popped off." Brett positioned himself between the last two bottles. Each of the other cut bottles stood in the exact same positions Jeff had placed them in. Brett's blows were so quick that the glass was sliced without being moved anywhere. "Torii then just poured the liquid out casually, as if nothing had happened. But I could see how much it had taken out of him."

Brett pivoted to the left and right in a lightning fast motion. He sliced the right bottle with his left hand and then the left bottle with his right. The right bottle fell into two as had all the others. The left bottle was cut perfectly, but it moved to the left a fraction of an inch. Brett swore under his breath. "Not perfect." Archer looked at the Ninja Master's hands. There was not a cut on them.

He finished positioning the newly lit candles and approached his own Sensei. "I cannot fathom how you do all that without a *kiai,*" he said in awe. That was the shout which concentrated the *ki* into a single blow. It was the "hi-ya!" producers made their movie actors say while delivering a karate chop and the high animal screech Bruce Lee made while fighting.

"Practicality," Brett replied, hopping nimbly up on the edge of the beer-splashed table. "A ninja doesn't eat large amounts of food and drink because he can't afford to have to shit at an important moment. So if I'm going to catch an enemy by surprise, I can't afford to scream in his ear."

Brett stood on the sides of his feet on the edge of the table. Archer stumbled back, his mouth open in amazement. Brett didn't just stand upright with all his weight on his feet edges, he put his feet parallel to the edge of the table and then stood as if all his weight was still on his soles. In other words, he was leaning straight out over the floor at an angle of about forty-five degrees, balanced perfectly to his left, leaning over the floor.

Jeff had seen the same thing done to comic effect in "The Wizard of Oz." The Tin Woodsman started leaning from side to side as if he were just about to fall over, but every time Dorothy and the Scarecrow ran over to catch him, he'd straighten and lean over to the other side. Only that was a special effect done with a wire to hold the Tin Woodsman up. Brett was standing that way without a wire. He straightened up in apparent magical fashion, his feet flat on the tabletop.

"I got the balance right a lot sooner than I learned how to get back up again," Brett commented, dropping to the floor.

Before Archer could answer, Brett ran as fast as he could right at the wall next to where the candles were now positioned. As Jeff watched, Brett reached the wall and kept running at top speed. Only now he was running *up* the wall. Halfway up the twenty-foot height, he stopped and stood. For a split second he was actually standing straight out on the wall, horizontal to the floor.

In that second, he twisted his body and slashed at the candles. The speed of the blow put them out. Then he dropped to his feet on the floor.

Archer was totally speechless for a few seconds. Finally he managed to stammer, "How—how will I ever—?"

"Only compete against yourself," Brett advised him simply. "Never against me. That was my biggest mistake for years. I always wanted to defeat my instructors. I always wanted to be as good as they were. I didn't realize that I had to be the best I could be, not the best they could be. It's the same with everything. Don't compete. Your will will be sapped. Just be excellent."

Archer stared at him for a couple of seconds in wonder, then said, "That's easy for you to say. You just climbed up the fucking wall!"

Brett laughed. "Let's go have dinner."

The Rhea Dawn was in Japan-Town, also known as Japtown or J-Town. But it was known by the latter names the same way the City by the Bay was known as Frisco. You could call it that, but you might get punched in the mouth by a resident in earshot. The restaurant was on the very edge of the sector, away from the main concentration of the Oriental eating spots.

It wasn't a diner and it wasn't a palace. It was a tastefully done spot decorated mostly in teak. Where it truly excelled was in the culinary department. Rhea and Hama, the two manager-cooks were concerned with authenticity, but they didn't think ancient menus were etched in stone. And they were totally indifferent to the standard tastes which dictated how one should translate Oriental into Occidental terms. They sweated over their stoves and served the best food they could prepare.

Brett and Jeff were at the one upstairs table cleverly positioned to look over the main floor without being seen. A narrow stairway on the side wall connected it to the large dining area while an electric dumbwaiter was its connection to the kitchen. Brett sat eating shrimp, reading the evening papers and talking with Jeff as the late-night dinner crowd was in full swing.

"It's a perfection of character," Brett said seriously, his mind on neither the paper or the food. He was thinking about the forty minutes between the end of his first life and the beginning of his second. At first the thought that he could have done something to prevent his family's murder tortured him. Even after his second, more advanced, ninja education, he couldn't forget about it completely, but he now regarded the tragedy philosophically.

"One cannot control outside events," Brett went on. "You cannot be everywhere at once. So you must control inside events through perfect self-control. And that requires perfect self-awareness. Through you, events can be controlled to a degree. But only to a degree. After that, you must be prepared for anything. Adaption is mandatory and constant."

"Easier to say than do," Jeff nodded. "To adapt you need to know hundreds of karate styles, and just as many akido, judo, tae kwon doe, and related martial arts styles; you need to learn the three hundred sixty pressure points; you need . . ."

"You need to know everything," Brett said flatly. "Life is what life is all about. You need to study everything about it if you are to end it."

Archer digested this information and his food in silence. Brett looked over his paper at the twenty-five-year-old man. Wallace assumed that Jeff must have guessed by now how serious the Ninja Master had become. Archer was one of three who knew who Brett was and what he could do, but he was the only one being trained by Brett in the way of the ninja. The price of failure in *ninja-do* was death.

The other two people who knew Brett's double identity appeared in the doorway and joined the men at the table. The first was Rhea Tagashi, a breath-taking Oriental beauty of twenty-seven years. Her face was that of an innocent, loving angel. She had the long, lustrous black hair Japanese women were famous for. Her eyes were deep and beautifully almond-shaped. Her lips were naturally rich and red. Her body seemed Westernized in that her breasts were wider and fuller than most of her countrywomen's and her body more muscular.

She was wearing her restaurant outfit of a wraparound print dress with a bright red and black design that seemed both Japanese and American at the same time. There was a sheen of thin sweat across her tan, smooth skin. She put one hand behind Brett's head and one on Jeff's shoulder. Brett leaned back to meet her lips as she leaned down. They kissed as Hama came into the room.

He was a blunt, bullet-shaped man with a naked head. As the mood hit him, he could look like a wonderfully happy little Confucius or Buddha type, or he could look like the Oddjob character from the James Bond movie "Goldfinger." As always, he was dressed in a T-shirt and karate pants. On his feet were straw slippers.

"Eleven o'clock already?" Jeff asked the cook as he flopped down into a chair. Jeff was alluding to the restaurant's closing time.

"Another day, another million sushi," Hama replied tiredly. "Time sure flies when you're having won ton."

"How did it go today?" Rhea asked Brett.

"The Crimson Knights will be a lot nicer to their elders in the future," Brett predicted.

"No trouble?" Rhea inquired further, her concern for him showing.

"So, great white hunter," Hama began, leaning across the table, his fingers intertwining, "what now?"

"Well, smart mouth," said Brett, leaning forward as well. "What do you know about gambling?"

"I can lose with the best of them," Hama replied. "You want in on a game in Chinatown?"

"I'm talking bigger stakes than that," Brett said.

"Ain't no bigger stakes than that," Hama interjected quietly.

"I'm talking Atlantic City," Brett summed up.

Hama leaned back and whistled atonally until the tune of "Here She Is, Miss America" could be discerned.

"It's time for another summit meeting, everyone," Brett announced. "Tomorrow morning I want to know what is going on in Atlantic City, New Jersey." He looked at his pupil. "Jeff, research the layout." He turned to Hama's unconcerned visage. "The usual," the Ninja Master told him. "Underground activity and gun count." He looked up at his associate and confidante. She looked at him with an expression of concerned affection. "Rhea," he said, "let's go to bed."

When she awoke, he was already at the computer.

From her vantage point in the northeast section of the loft over the Rhea Dawn, the Ninja Master's living area made her feel small and unimportant. On the east side of the floor was his large, carefully stocked kitchen, the self-enclosed bath area and the sleeping section. She sat up in the platform bed; the sleeping mat to her right, the water bed to her left. Brett could sleep anywhere at any time, but when he could sleep regularly, he liked variety.

On the west side of the room was the dining area, the wardrobe, and finally, taking up the most space, the research and entertainment section. The large, carefully programmed Nippon General (NEC) computer was on and silently coughing out information. This was the source of the police files that first put Brett onto the Crimson Knights' trail. He had spent months researching the machines, then many more months setting them up so that they "borrowed" information from other computers all over the country.

She saw the CB radio on its shelf above and to the left of the main computer console. Just below that was the police band unit. And beneath that, housed in its own standing console, was the giant sit-down ham radio unit. All the machines were tied into headphones as well as speaker devices which channeled the information in a coherent manner. They were all information gatherers which Brett used as a library, lawyer, doctor, teacher, and stool pigeon.

Brett was sitting before the large TV screen wearing gray slacks and a light blue shirt. On his feet, crossed on the bamboo mat in front of the towering gadgets, were blue pull-on deck shoes. His face had a slight blue-green glow reflected from the video screen. He turned toward Rhea as she leaned back against the bed's headboard. She was wearing only a satiny black teddy which accentuated all her physical pluses. Brett could not help smiling at her in appreciation.

She smiled back, honestly flattered that she could distract him from his intense information-gathering task. The data he learned might later save his life, so to capture his concentration this way was high praise indeed. Rhea rose languorously from the bed, stretching her long, slim limbs. She reveled in the bright, clear morning light which streamed in from the French doors to her left. Through them, she saw only sky. They were built so no other building could be seen. That way, no one else could see in.

She moved with her natural, unforced grace to the bathing area. Inside the opaque, smoky beige Plexiglas compartment was a bathtub, shower, redwood tub and steam room. Slipping off her teddy, she took a quick shower and pulled on her kimono. When she emerged Hama and Jeff had already arrived and were seated around the table. As Rhea moved unerringly to the kitchen to get their drinks, Brett moved from the chair in front of the TV to the chair at the table head.

"Jeff?" Brett said to get things rolling.

"Atlantic City is built on Absecon Beach, an island

60

about three-fourths of a mile wide and ten miles long. It can be reached by Route 87, Bacharach Boulevard; Route 30, Absecon Boulevard; Route 40-322, or by the Atlantic City Expressway. The Expressway and Albany Avenue are makeshift boundaries for the Bader Field Airport. The bus terminal is at Arkansas and Atlantic Avenues.

"The Boardwalk stretches for about seven miles along the ocean front, but is sixty feet wide. The beach is about a hundred fifty yards wide at high tide."

"So the distance from the casinos to the water is about a hundred seventy yards," Brett calculated as Rhea put glasses of fruit juice in front of him and Jeff, then approached Hama with a Bloody Mary. She didn't consider it "women's work" and neither did they. It was simply that they had done the research, so somebody had to get the drinks. If she was conferring with Brett, no one would think twice about becoming the servant.

As she set the red liquid down in front of the blunt cook, he spoke up. "All right, already, let's get to the good stuff."

Jeff smiled and took the cue. "There are about fifteen major hotel-casinos on the Boardwalk in various stages of completion. Even so, they are all located between Virginia Avenue and Albany Avenue along the waterfront, a distance of no more than three miles. The main bunch of some seven establishments are huddled between New York Avenue and Arkansas Avenue, a distance of less than a half-mile. They all lie between the Million Dollar Pier and the Central Pier and you can see almost all the others from whichever one you're at.

"Besides those two, there are the Ventnor Pier in Ventnor City, the Steeplechase Pier, the Steel Pier, and the Garden Pier near the edge of the Absecon Channel."

"Ventnor?" Hama exclaimed. "New York Avenue? It sounds like a damn Monopoly board."

"It is," Jeff retorted easily. "The Monopoly game was

based on the streets and layout of Atlantic City. All the Avenues are there—Atlantic, Mediterranean, Illinois, even Marvin Gardens. There's water everywhere, with the Atlantic on one side and a system of bays everywhere else. To the east, Absecon Inlet, to the north, Clam Bay and the Intracoastal Waterway. To the west, Little Bay, Duck Bay, and Newfound Bay. To the south, Lakes Bay and Great Island."

"Okay," said Brett. "Now we know where we are." He turned to Hama. "What's going on there?"

"Oh, the usual," Hama said casually as Rhea came from preparing a fruit juice for herself and sat to Brett's right. "All the sins flesh is heir to. Naturally the Mob is all over the place, ensconced in a variety of profitable, but highly legal pursuits which served the overall end. But ever since Frank Costello died, things have been kind of strange."

"Strange?" said Rhea. "Strange how?"

"From all outward signs, things are more controlled, organized, and businesslike than ever before. The legal pursuits are almost more worthwhile than the time-tested corruption. And they are certainly less hassles."

"But you can't teach an old dog—" Jeff began.

"And a leopard can't change his spots and all those other cliches," Hama completed for him. "Joe Columbo and Crazy Joe Gallo get shot, and all of a sudden there's no *capo di capo re*—Boss of All Bosses. The rest of the structure stayed pretty much the same. There's the co-existing Jewish and Italian families. There's a loose commission of regional leaders—getting looser with the passing of time and the flow of money—and then the hired help that's called in.

"The hired help was the first problem. With the success of 'The Godfather' film there was the little boy who wanted to be a policeman, the one who wanted to be a fireman, and the one who wanted to be a hit man. Thanks to the ever-burgeoning network news programs, the message that 'crime pays' grew all the more loud. Finally it became a matter of record that most of these Mob crimes went unpunished. It seemed the perfect business for an enterprising young sociopath to get into.

"These killers of every race and creed muddied the water somewhat. Then there are the factions outside the Mob who wanted a bigger slice of the pie with the advent of the equal rights movement. Blacks, Puerto Ricans, the Irish, even the Orientals started spreading out a bit. That caused a little more than friction.

"Once the rules were set, Miami and Las Vegas were open territories where everybody could have fun and any violence was immediately punishable by annihilation. Then all the big bosses were gone, gambling was legalized in New Jersey and everybody moved in, their shoulders rubbing uncomfortably."

"Sounds like a ticking bomb," Jeff commented.

"Snuffed out before the fuse could be lit," Hama corrected him. "The boys in the white hats knew the danger in Atlantic City being thought of as a Mob town. The tourists would stay away in droves. So the gambling side of it was cleaned out and the strictest possible rules set. Any whiff of Mob connection for a casino or hotel and the entire structure would be bodily removed and dumped inland."

"Besides," Rhea interjected. "Gambling was legalized. What could the Mob control, except drugs, let's say."

"Let's also say linen and cigarettes," Hama elaborated. "Let's say all the little things that make a hotel go round. The sheer amount of supplies necessary to run those seventeen casinos could keep one family rolling in dough for some time to come."

"Fifteen," Jeff corrected in return. "Fifteen casino-hotels."

"There's also prostitution," Brett finally added, rising from his seat. "That's a big, profitable market."

"No doubt," said Hama, watching Brett approach the computer console. "Only the best talent is shipped in and professionally set up. Of course there's always the enterprising entrepreneur who tries to set up shop in an alley, but he's usually shown the error of his ways very quickly."

Brett hit a button set into the arm of the easy chair in front of the TV screen. A newspaper clipping immediately appeared on the screen. The headline read "THREE PEOPLE FOUND DEAD." The gist of the article had two attractive young women and a well-dressed man found bound and shot in a van on the outskirts of Ventnor Heights.

"One bullet each," said Brett, turning to them. "In the back of the head. Practically the calling card in a Mob kill or professional hit. Is that what you mean by them being shown the error of their ways, Hama?"

"Not damn likely," the cook retorted. "That maneuver is too flashy. Its just what you said, a calling card. A warning to someone to get out or lay off."

"Sounds like a Mob war brewing," Jeff concluded.

"It's quite possible," Hama agreed. "When someone starts muscling in on someone else's territory or someone even thinks the other person might be thinking about muscling in, the cat-and-mouse game of threat and double-threat starts. It's all very civilized until the bullets start flying."

"They've started," said Brett. "All the signs are there and the bodies are piling up. The cops and papers, as always, are playing it close to the chest to protect themselves from a country-wide scare which could hurt the place, but there's been more than just this one instance. Even so, this is the only news leak that saw print. In a Connecticut newspaper. There was no follow-up report anywhere."

"So what are you going to do?" Rhea inquired seriously.

"Go in and clean the place up like Humphrey Bogart or Gary Cooper?"

Brett leaned over the chair and smiled. Rhea was playing the devil's advocate, he thought. She always did. She would ask questions until she was sure that *he* was sure about what he was doing and what he was doing it for.

"I just want to find one woman," he told her. "One who might be in a lot more trouble than she realizes. I want to get to her before the mob war does."

"A prostitute?" Jeff correctly guessed.

Brett nodded. "An innocent girl thrown out of her family because she got pregnant. I don't know what happened to the baby, but the mother is in Atlantic City selling her soul for a bank roll. Hama, what kind of thing does she, and I, have to look out for?"

"There are two main families diversifying," the cook informed them. "The Arrow and Testi families. Arrow wants it all. Testi wants to hold his own, but if Arrow gets in his way, he'll try to crush him."

"Who crushed these three?" Brett asked, waving his hand at the computer's news clipping.

"That's one for the ages," Hama replied indifferently. "No one's talking on the grapevine and no one's taking credit for the kills. As far as I know, they were two hookers and a pimp important enough to eliminate, not just shoo away. It may not even be connected to the main war."

"Then I'll have to find out," Brett said.

"Why bother?" Hama shrugged.

Everyone looked at the bullet-headed cook. It wasn't like him to be so callously apathetic.

"I mean it, Brett," he defended himself lightly, "what's the point. You know the phrase 'they only kill each other.' It's valid in this case. It is absolutely *verboten* to hurt an innocent bystander or kill an outsider. They know the wrath of the public would come down on them like a ton of bricks. So why interfere? Let them murder each other off for you."

Brett accepted Hama's suggestion in silence. He stood still and seemed to look through the people at the table for a second.

"Master Yamaguchi once told me that evil did not have to be seen," Brett said. "Evil is, evil exists. It is not seen, it is known. You said it yourself, Hama. Children want to grow up and be hit men. And they can live out their warped fantasies without punishment and be paid for it. How much is the going rate now? Twenty thousand dollars? How many with a Saturday Night Special or a .44 Magnum bought at the local sporting goods store will take ten thousand? Five?

"That's bad enough," Brett continued, coming around his seat and approaching the table, "but the worst thing is that most people accept organized crime. They figure its part of their lives anyway, so they have no choice but to accept it. But this girl's mother cares. She's guilty and lost and confused. I swore to help those as victimized as myself. I've saved this woman from some muggers, but I can't stop there. Her daughter is dancing right toward the edge of a cliff."

"But what can you do for her?" Jeff asked. "You can protect her, but for how long?"

"I can tell her that her mother cares. That she is still loved. That there's some place she can go if she wants to. That she doesn't have to be a hooker." Brett shrugged. "Then it's up to her."

Hama rolled his eyes, but Rhea rose from her chair, wrapped her arms around Brett's neck and kissed him warmly, without pretense. When she pulled away, she nodded in understanding. It wasn't much—finding a daughter for an old woman and just giving her a message of acceptance where there was none before—but Brett was

66

about the only person in the country who could or would do it.

"But how will you get in?" Hama asked being obvious about his concern. As far as he was concerned, the girl would laugh at Brett's message. "You'll be walking right into the middle of a mob war, looking for one of the warrior's slave girls. You can hardly expect to get anywhere disguised as a tourist."

Brett stood at the end of the table smiling. "I have spent almost three decades learning the deadliest arts in the world. With that kind of background, what do you suggest I go as?"

Hama looked around the table, hoping to find the answer there, only to look back at Brett with an elaborate shrug.

"Hama," Brett said. "Where do you hide a killer so he can't be seen?"

A look of sudden realization spread across the cook's face. "Among other killers," he guessed.

"Exactly," Brett answered. "I'll want a list of the East Coast hit men most likely to be hired by the warring clans. If anyone is going to send a killer after Vicki Kelly, I'll want to know about it."

That was a cue for the meeting to be adjourned. Hama got up to research the assassin list through his Chinatown contacts. Jeff checked his watch, said his good-byes and headed downtown to open the dojo. Only when he and Rhea were alone did Brett grow pensive—as if a sixth sense had set an alarm off in his brain.

"I only hope I'm not already too late," he said quietly.

# Chapter Three

George Arrow was being watched. As he moved throughout his territory in the Diamond Head hotel-casino, many pairs of eyes were centered on him. First, there were the gazes of his bodyguards, lieutenants, and associates who depended on him for their well-being. He was one of the "dinosaurs"—fitting the old-world underworld mold: wide, stocky, barrel-chested, and tough. His face looked like a bunch of boulders stuck together with eye sockets, nostril holes and a mouth slit burrowed in.

His hair was dark, short, straight, and slicked back on his egg-shaped head. There were deep lines on his wide brow which could have been character wrinkles or shallow scars. He was not a man anyone would be pleased to cross. He wore the finery of his position. There were big, jewel-encrusted rings on two of his fingers, one on each hand, and a magnificent watch with a black face and gold numbers. His dark suit was tailored perfectly.

All this was taken in by the second pair of eyes: those quiet, brown eyes of Donald Stillman. He was aptly named. As one of the most professional hit men on the East Coast, he made many people still with his talents. As a professional, he had a few special talents: thorough, so he knew everything about his target's habits and scheduled movements as well as the best possible means of escape after the hit; versatile, so he could get in almost anywhere and use many different types of weapons to kill; discreet, so he was more interested in a clean, smooth hit than trumpeting himself as the greatest thing going. Because of that, he was available only by the very best contacts. He only got the very best contracts. Therefore he was the perfect man to hire for the murder of a family boss. He was amoral and simply saw the job as a challenge.

The challenge was in killing George Arrow and getting away with it. Once he got out of town, he wasn't worried about repercussions. He was simply a soldier doing the job he was hired to do. Other Mob members would probably respect him for a kill well completed. And if any Arrow family members came around for revenge, well, that was their funeral.

Stillman had sat in his Diamond Head hotel room going over the facts again. He had studied Arrow's routine for a week now. It was time to get the job done. Every morning at seven, the Mob boss got up in his penthouse suite atop the hotel and had breakfast with his lieutenants as well as various political and private sector people he had in his pocket."

From nine to eleven he worked in his private office making and receiving calls that concerned business. At eleven he went down to the spa and spent a little time swimming, in the steam room, getting a massage—or all three. At twelve-thirty he called his girl friend and she

met him in the Diamond Head Tap Room for lunch. A
two on the nose, they left the hotel. Arrow dropped he
off at another apartment, then went on a regular tour o
his locations to confer with his people. At four-forty-fiv
he was back at the Diamond Head Gold Mine cocktai
bar and restaurant for a round of drinking and talkin,
with various businessmen. At seven o'clock his girl frien
was picked up and brought over so they could have dinne
until nine.

Then it was a show until eleven or one, when he woul
always go back up to his office to make and receive mor
calls from all over the country. There were many weal
spots in the schedule, but the man who had hired hin
was adamant about one thing. It wasn't to be a surprise
Arrow couldn't be shot or blown up without knowing wha
hit him. The kill had to be personal. He had to have
second to realize he was pinned.

Stillman didn't mind. Lord knew his client wa
paying enough for his services and the hit could hardl
be accomplished any other way. Arrow's car was bullet
proofed, so a sniper's rifle was out of the question. It wa
well guarded so a time bomb wouldn't work either. It ha
to be a close kill in the Diamond Head itself. He had t
chance by with a silenced weapon and be gone befor
Arrow and his men realized that he had been shot.

The assassin laid his various choices out on the bed
There was the Heckler and Koch HK-4 automatic or th
Mauser HSc. Both were sleek, small guns which could b
used in either a .32 or .380 caliber format. But both wer
esoteric imported models that could be traced to him eve
with all the stenciled data filed off.

So it had to be one of the classic hit man weapons
Either the Smith & Wesson silenced snub-nose with handl
taped or the two shot derringer which used balls instea
of bullets so they didn't have rifling which could b
studied. Either way, Stillman would brush by Arrow in

70

crowd, shoot him, and then dump the gun in a trash can on the way out. By the time the lieutenants mobilized and the gun was found, he'd be long gone.

Stillman got up from the bed and checked his appearance in the mirror. He saw a thirty-two-year-old man with an innocent face and a slightly receding hairline. The nose was small and the lips were regular and slightly turned up at the ends, making it appear that he always had a bit of a smile. It was a charming, trustworthy face. You could buy a used car from the man.

His clothes didn't belie the image. He was attired in good style, but not so well-dressed that he would stand out in a crowd. Even a woman attracted by his boyish good looks might usually have to look twice before actually appraising him. Stillman left his position in front of the mirror, packed away all the guns except the snub-nose and called room service to send up his lunch.

He had no intention of eating it, but he also had no intention of checking out. After Arrow was murdered, he was sure all the people leaving the hotel at that time would be checked. Stillman, registered under the false name Bill Langer, would check out the day after. He waited forty minutes for his meal to arrive, tipped the bellboy, and put his plan into its final countdown.

He took his one suitcase, complete with hidden compartments for the guns, and all the clothes he had needed, and packed it in a large box. He took the box to the post office where he sent it to a drop he knew of in Long Island. Then he returned to the hotel. Once he was in the lobby, he checked his watch. It was three minutes to two. Stillman began to make his way up the elevator, past some shops, across a foyer to the entrance of the Tap Room.

A final pair of eyes watched Don Stillman approach. They were the eyes of the man who had hired him. They were steel gray eyes.

71

Stillman didn't see Brett Wallace sitting on one of the foyer's sofas. The hit man didn't see him when he was watching him from the shops. He didn't see him at the taxi stand. For as innocuous as Stillman made himself look, Wallace could always do him one better. The Ninja Master was dressed in dark green and brown, camouflage colors that, among other things, blended in with the mezzanine carpets and upholstery. After cultivating the right stillness, Brett all but blended into the background.

It had been a long week for him as well.

Vicki's murder had changed the entire complexion of his mission. The errand of mercy was terminated by an act of vengeance. Brett was intent on punishing whoever had callously wiped out the life of the innocent girl. He had executed her assassins, yes, but now he had to find the person behind the kill orders. He had to discover which mob boss had targeted Vicki as a dead woman.

He did not have much time to plan. The Shop slaughter meant that the war was heating up. As quickly as possible, Brett had to get inside the fighting families, find out who had more to gain by Vicki's death, and then even the score.

It was a frustrating situation. He had spent his first Atlantic City days finding the girl, only to arrive at her side just minutes too late. But as soon as he had seen her lifeless body, he had stopped feeling remorse. His emotion now was one of conviction: the girl would not die in vain.

A fast call to Hama set his new plan into motion. The Ninja Master had hired a hit man. He spent fifty thousand dollars of his own money to rent a killer to kill George Arrow. Then he, in turn, tracked the man to make sure he didn't. And now it was all coming together here.

The cops had yet to be informed of the blood bath. Brett had rushed through the morning, getting some loose ends squared away. These loose ends had cemented his approach to this mission. He had to disembowel the Mob warriors from the inside. But first he had to get inside. Don Stillman would take care of that.

Brett got up at three o'clock. His body was practically attuned to that of both Stillman and Arrow. Stillman stopped looking at some Hathaway shirts in the window of a men's store and nonchalantly ambled toward the restaurant entrance. At that moment the elevator doors opened between Stillman and Brett so a crowd of hungry tourists could come out and head for the eatery.

Brett saw George Arrow amid a group of his men make their way from the dim Tap Room interior. He saw Stillman drifting over to the side of the open, thick red double doors of the entrance. He seemed to be moving very casually and slowly, but he was actually making his way right through the moving crowd of innocents to the front of the throng.

Arrow's soldiers came out first, automatically glancing in each direction. Stillman had attached himself to the side of the expectant lunchers and subtly turned away so that his face was not visible to the guards.

Brett had to hand it to the killer. He was certainly giving Wallace fifty thousand dollars worth. That was just the down payment. Their deal had been another fifty when the job was done. Brett had no intention of having to pay.

As the guard on the left looked back into the restaurant, Stillman looked back at the entrance. The way his head moved, he should have seen Brett amid the approaching, chattering group of innocents. The hit man's eyes passed right by as if seeing empty air. Brett didn't have to look away. He had positioned himself so that he was in Stillman's blind spot and behind a wider man. Brett's invisibility was made even more effective by the fact that he was the very last person Stillman would have expected to see.

Arrow's girl friend came out. She was looking back, but Brett could see that she was a truly beautiful, truly unconcerned blond. The kind of attractive creature only lots of money could buy. A rich white fur coat covered her body but it didn't take much imagination to fill in the curves.

Stillman's luck was impeccable. All the disparate groups reached the restaurant entrance at the same time. Stillman was moving right behind Arrow as he turned toward the elevator, his people on either side. He was walking past the entire group of innocents on his way, Brett being in the forefront. It was a perfect setup. Stillman would slip the gun out of his coat, swing it forward and around at the level of his hip so that it would shoot up into Arrow's chest from the side and just become one of the panic-stricken bystanders as the Mob boss crumpled and the soldiers went crazy.

Brett saw it begin to happen. After that, no two witnesses' stories were exactly alike. Only Brett knew what happened because he did it.

The gun was out and pointing when Brett shouted, "Watch it!" Even as the words got out, he was kicking with his left foot. As everyone tensed and Stillman's finger tightened on the hair trigger, Brett's foot was wrapping around the hit man's hand lengthwise. Wallace had left his loafer shoe on the floor as he kicked. The toes and sole acted as a hand with fingers to push the weapon away and point it where the bullet wouldn't hit any flesh.

It was really perfect, because the gun coughed and the lead went through a crease in Arrow's jacket before slamming into the edge of the open restaurant door. That was the best way of getting the Mob man's attention. Now Brett had to move just as fast to make sure the soldiers didn't capture Stillman alive. Still, the death could not be too unusual or outlandish. Wallace had to keep the knowledge of his "empty hand" killing skills to himself.

Brett leaped forward, jostling Arrow aside in the process. He grabbed Stillman's gun arm with both hands and drove him back against the wall. As they slammed into it,

Brett's left hand wrapped around Stillman's right, his forefinger pressing into a nerve just below the hit man's first knuckle. He threw his hand up, bringing Stillman's hand and gun with it. He pressed down on the hit man's nerve three times. The gun fired into the ceiling three times, so there was no mistake as to what was happening.

It was only then that Stillman himself began to understand what had gone wrong. Before that it seemed as if he had lost control of his limbs. He told them to do one thing and they did another. But then his eyes focused on the face in front of him and he bucked like a maddened rodeo bull trying to kill its rider.

Brett saw the look and gauged its effect. He had to keep Stillman quiet. Any dying message might cause him problems later on. Brett pulled the gun arm down as if he were playing with a GI Joe doll. He wrenched it around and pressed it against Stillman's stomach so that the barrel was between their bodies pointing up at the hit man's heart underneath his rib cage. Brett's other hand sunk its fingers around Stillman's neck. The hit man's shocked, angry expression stayed the same, but whatever he was intending to shout was locked in his throat.

Arrow had fallen onto the ground and was quickly shielded by his men. They pulled out their weapons to the instant hysteria of everyone in the foyer and restaurant. Even though some people were throwing themselves down and others were running in every direction, a couple of the bodyguards were able to get a bead on the two struggling figures.

"No!" Arrow shouted, twisting up to a sitting position and hitting the gun arms down.

Stillman's face added the expression of agony as Brett's fingers squeezed down. His free hand tried to beat at Wallace's head, but Brett would let go of his neck long enough to block the blows. Finally he pressed the trigger-finger nerve one more time. Completely against his will, Stillman felt his forefinger contract.

The hit man died immediately as the bullet soared up under his septum and ripped through his heart. He died not understanding how he could be dragged around like a rag doll. He died not understanding why the man who had hired him had killed him.

Brett jumped back and let the dead hit man slide down the foyer wall, his open eyes glassy and unseeing. A thin, solid line of blood was drawn on the wall as he dropped. Brett heard three hulking bodyguards charge him from the rear, but he forcefully kept himself from dropping them. He had to maintain his guise as a "normal" hood, so he let them jump him and manhandle the merchandise.

They clawed and pummeled him, searching for any weapon. Brett deflected the debilitating blows while taking the ones that wouldn't cause him any lingering harm. He watched, detached, as Arrow himself started digging through his men angrily.

"That's enough!" the Family head shouted as he pulled the men off. "I said that's enough!" He got the last guy off Brett and pushed them all away. "Can't you see this guy saved my life? He isn't going to hurt me!" Arrow stood in front of Brett, lecturing his men, as Wallace made a show of pulling himself together.

The Mob boss turned to Brett who was dusting himself off casually. "You alright, mister?" Arrow asked.

"Yeah," said Brett. "Your dogs not only bite too quick, they don't bite hard."

Arrow seemed to like what he heard which was a lot more than could be said about the guards. Any further conversation was called on account of Diamond Head security guards racing up the escalator and pouring out the elevator in large numbers.

"Tony," Arrow instructed the soldier nearest him, "you take Tamara home. Call me when she's safe. I'll be in my office." He turned back to Brett as Tony carefully took the stunning blond's arm and led her across the foyer. "What's your name, mister?"

"Sullivan," Brett replied. "They call me Shack."

"All right, Mr. Sullivan," said Arrow, taking his arm and leading him away from the waves of Mob guards explaining to the hotel's guards what had happened, "I owe you a debt of gratitude. You want to come up to my office for a couple of minutes?"

Arrow was putting his words into action even as he was saying them. He guided Brett unerringly toward the elevator, its doors still open after the guards had left. He was not a man to say "no" to.

"Sure," said Brett. "I could use a couple of seconds to catch my breath."

"Fine," said Arrow, motioning for him to go into the enclosure first. The Mob boss followed him in a second later, along with three of his men.

Brett placed himself in the left rear corner of the elevator while one of the men took a key Arrow handed to him. The key was placed in a lock behind a small door beneath the control buttons. Beneath the lock was another button. The guard turned the key and pushed the button. The door closed and the car surged upward, stopping at none of the hotel's many floors.

After it had passed the last number etched in the directory above the doors, the car finally stopped and the doors opened into a small office lobby. There was a desk right in front of them, closed double doors behind that, a sofa to the left and a coffee table covered with magazines to the right. A pretty, dark-haired girl in a white uniform sat behind the desk. It looked like the anteroom of a dentist's office.

When the girl saw Arrow, her placid expression turned to surprise and then concern. "Is everything all right, Mr. Arrow?" she asked nervously, beginning to get up.

"Everything's fine, Angie," he replied, walking out first with his hands in a calming gesture. "Could you call my appointments for this afternoon and set up another time with them?"

Angie plopped her firm bottom down on her padded seat. "Certainly, sir," she said, all business again. To the untrained eye she did not move once she had reseated herself, but Brett saw that both her right hand and left foot moved in unison. The hand must have touched a button on the lip of the top drawer while the foot must have hit a switch on the floor. It was a double lock system which opened a section of the right wall between a potted plant and the magazine table.

One guard went first, followed by Brett, followed by another guard, followed by Arrow, trailed by the third guard. They made a strange parade into a hallway with two doors on each side and a final door at the end. Arrow took the lead in order to open the second door on the right. All five went into a sumptuously decorated office.

Arrow moved toward the large desk situated in front of a window which looked out over the ocean. Two of the men stayed by the door while the third stood to the right of the desk. Brett had a lot of chairs to choose from. There was another sofa to the left, three chairs in front of the desk, and a table surrounded by chairs in a small dark section off to the right. Brett walked over and sat on the right end of the couch.

Arrow was prepared for him to sit in one of the high-backed, plush red and brown chairs, so he pivoted his large throne to his right on its four wheels, a look of slight consternation on his face. Then the expression cleared into one of appreciation. Here was a man who was different, his expression clearly said.

"Why don't you sit where I can see you better?" Arrow baited, motioning to the chairs.

"I like to see what I'm up against at all times," Brett said easily.

"What makes you think you're up against anything?" Arrow returned casually, busying himself with papers on the desk.

"I'm always up against something," Brett shrugged. "It's the nature of the game, like . . ." He waited until Arrow looked over at him, and finished the sentence. ". . . what happened downstairs." Brett delivered the sentence with a sharklike smile.

Arrow smiled back like a whale who had eaten whole schools of sharks in his lifetime. "That's right," he remarked. "As I said before, I owe you a debt of gratitude, Mr. Sullivan. I think it's safe to say you saved my life. I consider myself fairly generous with those who do me a service and I value my life very highly. With those criteria set, is there anything I can do for you in return?" The Mob boss delivered the speech like a school principal offering a free "A."

"Yes," said Brett. "You can let me continue to be of service to you. You could let me in on the action."

Arrow continued to smile blandly at Brett. He held that pose for a moment, then said "I'm not sure I understand. What makes you think I have any action to share?"

Brett coughed, then let his head roll back. "Anybody who could walk away from a murder attempt with no questions asked is more than your average, everyday, run-of-the-mill businessman," he said to the ceiling. "If you're important enough to kill, then believe me, you've got some action I want to be in on."

Arrow leaned back, considering what Brett had said. He made a steeple with his fingertips touching each other and leaned back. "Just who are you, Mr. Sullivan?" he asked amiably.

"I'm nobody," Brett answered honestly, rising from the sofa and approaching the desk. He could sense the guards tensing at his movement. "Just a Joe who recently got Stateside with no money but some contacts."

Arrow watched him carefully. "What does that mean?" he asked as Brett leaned between two high-backed chairs.

"It means that I know who you are, Mr. Arrow and I know what's going on around here," Brett said point blank. "Come on, Mr. Arrow. With all due respect, you think I just happened to be passing by downstairs? I knew the hit was going down and I knew that I could prosper by stopping it."

Arrow folded his hands on his stomach and rocked gently back and forth. "It did occur to me that your appearance was no accident, Mr. Sullivan," he said. "That's why I brought you up here more than anything else. But my question to you is how could you have known about the assassination . . ." Arrow held onto the end of the word, then summed up by pointedly adding, . . . "attempt?"

"It's as I said before," Brett answered. "Contacts. It's fairly common knowledge on the underground grapevine that you and Testi have a beef." Brett moved slowly around to the front of the middle chair. "After a little more looking, I filled in the details." He stood right in front of the desk.

"Details?" Arrow asked innocently.

Brett felt them coming through his feet. Although they were silent, he felt each one of the guards' slow footsteps coming up behind him through the carpet. To Brett's ninja-developed senses, it was as if the deep pile were telegraph wires sending the message right into his brain. He could picture their progress exactly.

"No big offense to your clowns, here," Brett said pointedly, looking over at the guard behind the desk. He felt the men behind him stop as well, "But you need a man like me to protect your interests." With that, Brett fell back into one of the chairs. He crossed his legs and arms with a big smile. He felt the men behind him start moving forward again.

"A man like you," Arrow echoed, keeping his gaze rock-steady on Brett so he would return the stare. "I repeat, Mr. Sullivan. Just who the hell are you and why should I trust you?"

"I'd like to tell you," said Brett. "I really would, but I don't have a past anymore. I got rid of it when I became a mercenary. I spent a couple of years fighting in a bunch of godforsaken hellholes around the world until I was captured in Africa. I spent ten years in their stinking jail getting tortured daily. Somewhere along the line I got amnesia. I forgot all about me and nobody seems to be able to tell me anything more about my life in the States. I got the name Shack because I spent most of my time chained in what they considered the cooler—a hut where they baked you before beating you."

"And Sullivan?" Arrow asked, getting interested.

"It's stupid, but I got the last name because I kept remembering Ed Sullivan saying 'Good night! Drive safely!' at the end of all his shows."

Arrow laughed.

"I told you it was stupid," Brett grinned. "But the one thing I learned over there was how to kill. I killed the other prisoners to stay alive. I killed all the guards to escape. I killed everyone in my way to escape. I cut a path across the bush. I lived like, and fed on, animals. Sixteen years in that kind of environment could change anybody. When I got back here, no one could tell me anything about who I was. Not doctors, not shrinks, not the police."

It was a pretty story and Arrow was impressed. He grinned the shark-killer grin again and leaned forward conspiratorily. "I don't like a man I've got nothing on," he said honestly.

"Give it time," Brett quipped back. "You'll find something." He eased himself deeper into the chair's padding. He knew that the two guards were flanking him behind the chair.

"Very interesting," Arrow admitted. "And very convincing. You've told me who you are, but you still haven't told me why I should trust you."

Brett shrugged minutely. "Actions speak louder than words," he said. No one was prepared for his next action, because everyone thought he was referring to the assassination attempt downstairs. So the guards were taken completely by surprise when he hurled the chair and himself backwards.

The tall, strong backing crushed down on the two guards' outside feet when he landed and even as that was happening, Brett was rolling back and slapping his hands flat on the floor. He did a handstand with a strong jerk, sending his heels into each guard's chin. As they stumbled back, he dropped into a crouch on his feet, grabbed the back of each man's knee and pushed. Both fell down hard.

Then, all he had to do was snake his hand between the flailing arms of the man to his left, pull the gun out of the guard's shoulder holster and shoot the third guard right through the protecting fallen chair.

The third guard swung back against the wall, his own weapon flying out of his hand and clattering across the conference table. As Brett quickly rose, he pulled the gun out of the last man's holster. He straightened, pointing one weapon at the ceiling, the other at the floor. "See what I mean?" he concluded.

As punctuation, the door slammed open and three more guards piled in, guns drawn.

"Get the hell out of here!" Arrow roared. "And take the rest of these assholes with you!" The Mob boss waited until the fallen men got to their feet and the shot man was lifted up and dragged out.

Just before the last men went out the door dejectedly, Brett called to them. "Hey." They looked back. "Catch," he said, throwing the guns to them. One bobbled the catch before both looked at him with napalm in their eyes. Brett just smiled and smiled. He waited until they closed the door after them before turning back to Arrow.

"I could have shot them all and I could have shot you," he said. "You want to talk any more about trust?"

"Please, Mr. Sullivan," Arrow said expansively as if he were talking to an entirely different man and nothing had happened. "Do sit down."

Brett complied.

"Very nimble," Arrow commented. "Very athletic. And very accurate. You shot him in the shoulder through a chair that was blocking your view."

"He'll live," Brett estimated. "You learn a lot in the African bush, Mr. Arrow. You learn how to use your wits, how to use your body and, when you have a gun in your hands, how to make the bullet go where you want it."

"I owe you my life," Arrow concluded. "Twice. You have convinced me that you would be a worthwhile addition to my personal staff. So, tell me. How can you be of service?"

"Well, sir," Brett replied humbly, "it seems to me as if somebody was trying to kill you. I think it might be a good idea for you to hire somebody he doesn't know to kill him before he kills you."

There were still some surprises left in life. Brett Wallace, now firmly established in his disguise as mercenary amnesiac Shack Sullivan, had utilized some of his ninja arts of psychology to control the conversation and pull Arrow along the mental path Brett wanted him to follow. But the Family head was not easy to lead. Try as he might, he could not convince Arrow to send him after Testi. The Mob boss was too good a businessman for that.

Instead he sent him to kill the Atlantic City head of prostitution, a person named Arcudi. Brett had been told that Arcudi was located at the Citadel, one of four well-organized whorehouses within the confines of the city. This Brett already knew. He had been avenging witness to the bloody closing of the Shop the night before.

It all fit in. The name Brett had gotten from that head hit man was "Arrow." The Mob boss must have already gotten word on what a mess that job had turned out to be, so he was even more receptive to Brett's appearance and talents. So now he was sending Shack Sullivan out to continue the job Flanaghan and his cronies couldn't do.

Brett and Arrow had hammered out their working relationship for the rest of the afternoon. As far as he was concerned, Sullivan was just hired help—an outside man to do the dirty jobs perfectly. That suited Shack just fine, since he charged premium prices for his services and collected half up front. By dinner time Brett came away from the Diamond Head with twelve thousand five hundred dollars in untraceable cash. He kept it in a small duffel bag.

Wearing the same dark green, military-cut shirt and the dark brown slacks with matching loafers he had on that afternoon, Brett walked along the Boardwalk toward the Million Dollar Pier.

It was no longer worth that much. Nowadays it looked about a dollar ninety-eight. The steel and wood structure was lined with rundown amusements, rides, and attractions which were all dark and closed. The paint was flaking, the metal was rusted and the wood was rotting. This was the Atlantic City where gambling was an illegal sin completely owned by the Mafia, the Atlantic City where the first Cosa Nostra Commission was called in 1929 to set policy, the Atlantic City resort spot with a population of sixty thousand and a yearly tourist count of sixteen million. Today the former number was probably halved and the latter number was at least tripled. And when each of those millions of people dropped a thirty-dollar minimum profit into the casino-hotel's coffers, that's a criminally large amount of money. A criminal-*making* amount of money.

Brett took his little hunk of that cash and hung a right onto Indiana Avenue. Like the race-car player in Monopoly, he went straight past Pacific, Atlantic, Arctic, Baltic, and Mediterranean Avenues before he came to the address of the Citadel. It was a lovely, old, remodeled and reinforced Victorian home on a side street—just like the Shop. It was the kind of white, shuttered, wood-sided, lace-curtained place where one might expect to find a rich old lady and her one thousand pet cats.

Brett trotted right up the steps, strode across the porch and knocked on the wooden door. There were two thin, stained-glass windows on either side of the door. Through those Brett noticed the shadows of several figures.

"May I help you?" came a voice from a tiny, well-disguised speaker beneath the doorbell. It was a male voice.

Brett didn't bend down and talk right into the button. He spoke up at the door normally, as if it were a person. "I'm not tired or poor," he said cheerfully. "But do you have any huddling masses yearning to be free?"

"Do you have an appointment?" said the voice, refusing to react to his Miss Liberty act.

Brett looked quickly around. He spotted the camera nestled in the shadows made by two interconnecting porch roof beams off to his right. He unzipped the duffel and held it open to the lens. "Do I need one?" he asked.

The door opened. Brett entered. There was a little foyer where the patron could hang his hat and coat next to another big door with no window and no knob on Brett's side. As he took that in, it swung open to reveal a beautifully restored old-fashioned sitting room, the kind rustic old inns might still have and the kind the best early twentieth-century hotels used to have. Right in front of Brett was a stairway built into the wall leading up to the right. Beneath that structure was a sign-in desk with no register. Behind the desk was a middle-aged man who looked like an insurance salesman.

That image was reinforced when the man came around the desk with an attache case in his hand. It was a thick, much-used vinyl case. The man motioned Brett over to some comfortable easy chairs which flanked an early-American style table. Without a word, the man set the case on its side, clicked open the clasps, and pulled it one quarter open. A screen filled the inside space and clicked into place. Brett was looking at a portable slide projector—the kind real estate men used on their house calls.

But instead of homes and policies, this projector rolled pictures of women. They were beautiful women, expertly photographed. They were extremely tasteful, very sensuous nudes, ones worthy of publication in the very best magazines.

Brett had to admit to himself that it was a very clever setup. The name and price of each girl was at the bottom of the picture. That way no incriminating words would be spoken and if a raid ever occurred, the evidence would go up with a flick of a Bic.

The show was very short. Only six girls were available, but each had much to commend them. As soon as the man had gone through them once, he went through them again, waiting for Brett to either shake his head or nod. He let Linda, Nancy, Kristine, Claire, and Karen, reluctantly, go by, before he decided on Cyndi. The middle-aged man nodded, closed the case, returned to the desk and retrieved an old-fashioned key—the kind with only two teeth. Attached to the ring at the other end of the key was an oval piece of brass with the number "6" engraved into it. Brett gave him money for it.

Brett was impressed. This place was worthy of the money spent in it. Without a bit of verbal communication, he went up the stairs into a quiet, dim, candlelit hall. The stairs ended in the middle of the second floor. There were three doors to the right and the same number to the left. Two of the six doors were on one wall, two on the other and one each at the ends of the hall. Brett looked to his right. The door at the end of the hall had a cameo in the center with the number "2" painted in a delicate design. To his left was a door with the number "5."

Brett walked to his left, the key in one hand and the slightly depleted duffel bag in the other. To the right of the fifth door was the one he was looking for. Brett stood in front of it for a few seconds, adjusting his senses to the sounds within. As far as he could tell, there was no army of goons waiting inside. Either the Citadel hadn't heard about the Shop's slaughter or it was still business as usual despite it.

As far as he could tell, only one woman waited within, in the company of a thick, soft bed; tall, thin open windows, and a lot of rustling lace. Brett thought it would be tacky to kneel down and look through the keyhole, so he trusted his instincts, slipped the key into the lock and turned. The tumblers gave with no resistance. He turned the perfectly cut crystal doorknob and pushed the partition open onto a dream.

Cyndi was better looking in person. She was an extraordinarily fresh faced natural blond who managed to look experienced and innocent at the same time. She also looked intelligent and capable—that was one of the reasons Brett had chosen her. If he was going to have sex with someone, he'd rather have it with someone he appreciated or respected . . . not to mention someone beautiful.

He knew Cyndi was beautiful immediately. The other qualities he'd find out soon enough. She stood five feet, seven inches tall with one knee on the brass bed and the other foot on the floor. Her hair flowed down to her shoulders in flaxen wisps. She wore only a floor-length white lace nightgown which rippled from the night wind breezing in from the open window behind her. She was illuminated only by moonlight, the candles in the hall, and a very dim oil lamp which bathed the room in shadows of black and gold.

A weaker man would have fallen to his knees and pledged everlasting servitude.

Brett couldn't help but smile. It was a lovely product, wonderfully packaged. Cyndi held her position for a second, then brought her other foot to the floor. With practiced grace and speed, she walked toward Brett, letting her gown sweep back behind her. It was a sensually cunning move, which revealed her smooth, cream-colored chest, most of her strong, round breasts and her long, shapely legs which appeared out of a slit in the gown dress.

She raised her arms slightly to hold his shoulder with one hand and his hip with the other, but he nimbly reached for the first hand and brought it to his lips. At the moment he kissed it, he also squeezed a nerve which sent a slight, electric-like shock up her arm. Not enough to hurt, but enough to give her a tingle she probably never felt before.

Brett enjoyed her reaction. The mixture of the tingle and his chivalrousness confused her for a second. She was used to lust, not tenderness. She was also taken aback by the unusual sensation. She thought she had felt it all and any kind of personal pleasure was long behind her. It was an odd overture that frightened her for a moment. Then the professional hooker returned to the fore. Again it was all business and acting out the fantasy.

She took his hand and led him toward the bed. Brett smiled warmly at the back of her head. It would be his great pleasure to break down that prostitute shell she had built up around her and get to the unloved woman inside. Without making an abrupt move, Brett swept in and smoothly lifted her up into his arms.

Cyndi couldn't stifle a small exclamation of surprise. She didn't know where she was or what had happened momentarily. She had hardly felt his arms. It was just as if she had suddenly learned to float. She found herself against Brett's chest, her right hand on her lap and her left hand resting lightly on his shirt. Initially she was afraid again and pushed with her left palm. Then she realized that he was holding her without effort. And it felt good. She added tender strength to politeness in her mental estimation of this gray-eyed, sandy-haired "john."

It wasn't as if she hadn't been carried before. But before it had been a "King Kong" carry, a bruising, frenetic half-tackle by some whooping Texan who hurled her on the bed and then leaped on top of her. This man carefully brought her over her silk-and-down-covered mattress and tenderly . . . slowly . . . draped her across it. His control was magnificent. He treated her as if she had no weight and there was no gravity. Throughout, his movements remained smooth; there was no sudden muscle spasm or fiber vibration.

Her head rested on the pillows, her blond mane making an angelic halo around her face. She reached up to wrap her hands around his neck. He caught them again and slowly laid them at her sides. Now she was getting a little pissed. It seemed as if he were consciously keeping her from doing whatever she wanted to do. But Cyndi forgot about that when he sat on the edge of the bed and leaned over her. The expression on his face seemed to go right through her skin and into her heart. It was the look of honest affection, appreciation, and serious interest. He cared about her, not just for his own desires.

She had it timed. He was going to lean in and kiss her. As their lips seemed destined to meet, she opened hers and got her tongue ready. At that moment, Brett stopped. She was all set. Her eyes were closed and her suction was on automatic. When his lips didn't show, she was thrown off. In surprise, she lost all her professionalism and opened her eyes. *Then* he kissed her.

As she might have expected, it was a warm, strong, giving kiss. One part of her mind tried to be cynical about it, telling her that he was just another sad rube who was making love to his mother image. The other part of her mind told the first part to shut the fuck up and enjoy it.

From her lips, Brett started concentrating on the rest of her body while nimbly taking off his own clothes. Disrobing always seemed to be the most awkward part of sex. Brett had that beat with his total muscle control, double-jointedness, and ability to silently dislocate his own bones for a second. The clothes seemed to peel off him of their own accord as he caressed Cyndi with his lips and fingers. As he progressed, she found herself more and more helpless. Even if she wanted to respond in a classically whorish manner, she found she couldn't.

Waves of light-headedness assailed her. Her arms felt weak, soft and heavy. Sensations she never felt before—and sensations she never felt before with such strength and clarity—were bombarding her overwhelmed libido almost all at once. As much as she knew about the human body, she didn't know that there were at least three hundred sixty pressure points across it that could cause pleasure, pain, or death—depending upon how pressure was applied.

Brett Wallace knew. To the ninja he had become, everything was an art and everything was a weapon, even sex. Unlike most of the practitioners, Brett knew exactly what to do and how to do it. But unlike most of his other abilities, this art needed the participation of another to be totally successful. So Brett invited Cyndi's experience and desires to come to the fore in the way he continued.

Their lovemaking was vigorous and exciting and culminated exactly an hour later. Brett had orchestrated it that way. And as the last note was sounded, Brett gently rubbed her neck, sending another wave of light-headedness over her which ended in a soft, dark blanket covering her mind. Cyndi went to sleep effortlessly, happier than she had ever been since childhood.

Another job well done, Brett thought humorlessly. Even if the girl remembered this evening with fondness, it was still only an hour of consideration out of a life which demanded pessimism, cynicism, and degradation. She was a prostitute serving idiots under a Mafia leader. Brett's job now was to find that boss.

He dressed quickly and went to the window. He looked out, seeing what appeared to be a quiet residential street with the large houses separated by picket fences and walls of elm trees. He also noted that the trees around the Citadel were cunningly pruned so that no limb grew too close to any of the windows. Looking down he spied several electric-eye devices situated near ground level. No one could approach the house from the side or back without being spotted. Brett also noted that the outside wiring was protected by little half-tubes of steel which covered them. That way, no one could cut the wires from a distance so they could approach the house without tripping the electric eyes.

Looking up, Brett saw several small cameras peering in every direction down the streets. They were attached to the roofing and must be giving someone pictures of the road activity. If a carload of hoods suddenly pulled up, the Citadel would know about it and be prepared. Brett wondered how long the cameras had been in use. He certainly hadn't seen any at the Shop.

He leaned back inside, took his duffel and went downstairs. Standing on the last step, he leaned over so the deskman could see him, held up enough money to pay for another hour and threw it over. Then he made an A-OK sign with his fingers, followed by a fanning motion as if to cool himself off. The deskman nodded knowingly. No other words had to be spoken.

Brett went back upstairs, thinking about his approach. The Citadel was fairly well covered from the outside. If a team of hit men approached, they could hold their own. But they were not prepared for a single assassin. And why should they be? There was no one that they were aware of who could infiltrate, get by all the safe guards and into the lair of Arcudi successfully. They were about to meet someone who could.

Brett went back into Cyndi's room, where she was still sleeping peacefully. He went to each side wall, listening intently for any movement. According to the vibrations, someone was in room one with Linda. Karen in room five sounded to be reading by the long pauses then the sudden crinkle and flap of pages. The walls were not thin. In fact, they were well constructed and practically soundproof. It was just that Brett had developed all his senses to an extreme degree.

Satisfied things were quiet, he approached the window once more while reaching deep into the duffel, below the money. His hand emerged holding a set of *shuko*—the opposite of brass knuckles, these were "palm claws." They were a band of metal and leather that, when slipped over the hand, secured four small hooklike claws in a person's palm. It was like having two sets of climbing fingers on each hand. What the digits couldn't navigate or support, the hooks could.

Brett reached outside, grabbed the top frame of the window and started climbing, coming up behind the cameras. As soon as he had approached the Citadel an hour or so ago, Brett had noted the similarities between it and the Shop. The interior layout was roughly the same as well. So logic dictated that Arcudi's office would be in either the basement or the attic. Brett was betting on the attic since it was a lot harder to reach and a lot easier to defend.

The claws worked perfectly on the wooden outside walls. To him, everything had a gripping surface, no matter how smooth it looked. Even so, its consistency dictated how he would circumvent its obstruction. In this case, it was as easy as climbing a tree to him. He sat down on the sloping roof within seconds of leaving the room. He looked over his shoulder at the infrared cameras peering down either side of the street. Keeping out of their wide-angle lenses' sight lines he walked to the opposite end of the roof, fell forward, grabbed the roof edge and leaned the top half of his body over the side.

He heard voices coming out through a shuttered small window. At first he thought he misoriented himself because one of the voices sounded female, but as he listened closer, the voices melded into a single angry male voice.

"You think *I'm* crazy?" the voice was saying incredulously. "You're sitting there with Arrow after you, killing your girls, scaring off your clients, buying off your protection, and you think I'm crazy for wanting to do anything about it?"

From what he was saying and how Brett heard it, the Ninja Master figured that the speaker was standing in front of Arcudi's desk between the shuttered window and Brett's target. From experience, he had to assume there was at least two other men in the room who served as guards. There was no way of telling that for sure without taking a look, and Brett wasn't going to blow his element of surprise by doing that.

Instead he checked the shutter. It consisted of several thin wooden slats lying atop one another horizontally.

From the color of the light reflected on the slats from within, Brett assumed that there was a small stained glass window behind it. Judging from this rainbow light and remembering the attic window sizes at the Shop he figured there would be just enough room for him to fit through feet first.

It was the only way to fly. Brett pulled his torso up, turned over and then lowered his body down, his fingers and the *shuko* implements digging into the roof ledge. He planted his feet on either side of the small shutter, bent his knees, and then pushed out. As he swung up like a trapeze artist, he brought his legs together, making a straight battering ram ending in his feet. Then he swung himself down again with all the speed his arms and shoulders could muster.

His feet went right through the slats and the glass as if they were breaking through paper, cardboard, and gelatin. The tinkle of the shattered glass hadn't even finished sounding when Brett drew his feet back and pulled his head forward and down to look into the room before he had landed.

His mind registered what his eyes saw even as his limbs were moving again. He did not kick the man in front of the desk forward. He landed behind him and grabbed his shoulder with his left claw at the same time. The *shuko* hooks dug into the man's shoulder, creating an unshakable grip. He threw the man backward into the guard to his left while swinging his right arm, palm up, into the face of the guard behind to his right.

The hooks sunk in and the man's scream was abruptly cut off when Brett tore down and pulled the man's gun out of his holster inside his jacket. The right guard was crumpling as Brett was moving forward and firing at the same time. He was vaulting across the desk as the bullet punched into the chest of the guard behind Arcudi's chair. That man was reaching into his own coat when he was hit so he never reached his gun. He slid to the floor as Brett landed behind the desk and hauled the chair away so Arcudi couldn't get a weapon or tap any buttons.

Brett swung the chair so the seated figure was facing him. He stuck the gun into the face before him and shouted at the two men he had originally thrown together.

"One move and . . ." he started before he realized that his gun was pointed at the small nose of a beautiful woman.

". . . *she's* dead," he finished.

# Chapter Four

His initial impressions had not been incorrect. He had heard a feminine voice inside the office. The room was approximately the same design as the attic in the Shop, only it was filled with business material rather than nursery stuff. And now it was filled by a shot guard, a moaning man with his face torn to ribbons, two amazed men picking themselves off the floor, a tense woman clutching the arms of her chair, and a calm man with a gun in her face.

"What are you waiting for?" she whispered to him. Brett didn't look over at her. He was looking everywhere at once although his eyes weren't moving. He was staring into space somewhere between her and the two men finding their feet. He saw all of them just fine. Arcudi was a small woman, about five feet, four inches tall, befitting her Italian heritage, but she was very attractive and well built.

Her face was round but not big, her hair was dark brown and wavy, and her eyes were olive. She was wearing a sweater, slacks, and a matching jacket.

The man Brett had thrown into the guard, the man who had been berating Arcudi about Arrow was a different kettle of lasagna. He was tall, gaunt, and gray-haired with a prominent brow and burning eyes. He was elegantly dressed in a perfectly tailored suit. He rose to his full height before speaking with barely contained rage.

"You must be insane!" he declared. "You'll never get out of here alive! You'll never get away with this!"

The man's angry words drew Brett's gaze to him. The Ninja Master's face was expressionless and distant for a second, but it suddenly changed into one of friendly indifference.

"Away with what?" Brett inquired lightly, tossing the gun onto the desk with loose fingers. "This is just my way of saying hello."

He had been listening for the sound of any other guards charging up from downstairs. He sensed no one. He had to assume that the Citadel kept a skeleton crew and the office was completely soundproofed.

Almost as soon as the gun clattered on the desk, the one unscathed guard started clawing for his holstered weapon. At first, it seemed as if he had Brett dead to rights. The time it took him to draw the gun out, aim, and fire was hardly enough to allow anyone to protect himself. But the gaunt man and Arcudi watched as Brett leaned over in a deceptively slow manner, picked up the dropped gun and shot the aiming guard in the forehead.

The man's head snapped back as the room was filled with another cracking retort followed by the wet smack of a bullet fired point-blank into a man's brain. It was a .32 caliber shell and didn't have enough drive to come splattering out the other side. The guard slammed against the

97

far wall, his arms flailing. His own gun went off once, the lead harmlessly hitting the ceiling.

The room was stunned into near silence—except for the moaning man with the shredded face. Brett let the gun drop back onto the desk as he straightened up beside the young woman. She was the one who finally spoke up, showing remarkable poise in her choice of words.

"If that's how you say hello," she told him huskily, looking right into his eyes, "I'd hate to see how you say good-bye."

Brett put his hands up in a loose surrendering position. "Self-defense," he explained calmly. "I wanted to see Arcudi without a lot of red tape."

"You're seeing her," she replied, beginning to relax. "I'm the Arcudi you're looking for. Angelina Arcudi." She boldly put out her hand.

Brett took it. "Shack Sullivan," he told her. They shook.

The gaunt man had watched the whole conversation with increasing expressions of disbelief. Finally his eyes had widened and his mouth had opened as far as they would go.

"This is preposterous!" he exploded. "Angelina, you're talking to a man who just burst in here and killed two of your men!"

Both Brett and the girl looked at the old man. "What would you suggest I do, Neal?" she asked. "Dance with him?"

"Killing two guards who were going to kill me is a far sight better than what I was hired to do," Brett informed him.

"And what was that?" Angelina asked quietly.

"Ms. Arcudi," Brett replied, looking down at her. "It appears that George Arrow wants a piece of your prostitution pie, and he is willing to kill you to get it. Now it seems to me that it might be a good idea if you kill him before he succeeds."

Now it was Arcudi's turn to surprise Brett. Almost as soon as Brett had finished, she replied smoothly and with some sardonicism.

"He doesn't want a piece, Mr. Sullivan, he wants the entire pie factory. And in terms of ending Mr. Arrow's life and thereby the threat he poses, that was the very thing Mr. Duggan was suggesting when you interrupted us."

Brett looked over at the tall man clenching and unclenching his fists. "And what did you decide?" Brett inquired.

"Angelina decided that murder was a lot more difficult than it seems," Neal Duggan answered.

Brett shrugged. "Security can be breached."

"It is not just the physical roadblocks that are stopping me," Arcudi said clearly. "There are the mental ones as well. You see, Mr. Sullivan, George Arrow is my father."

"Arcudi was my mother's maiden name," Angelina explained, taking the foil pan out of the oven with pot holders. "After the big break, I wanted to disassociate myself from my father, so I had it changed legally." She put the serving pan down on the aluminum table between Brett and Duggan. With a flourish, she pulled off the aluminum foil covering. A cloud of tomato-and-cheese-flavored steam rose up to the high kitchen ceiling.

*"Voila,"* she said. Duggan cried, "Ah!"

They were in the Citadel's kitchen, which was designed the same way the Shop's was. The men had been cleared out and the mess cleaned up in the attic before the main contingent of sex-starved clients appeared. It was business as always as Angelina suggested they all chat over dinner.

"The 'big break?'" Brett inquired as she went to a cupboard for some plates.

"Angelina's mother, Lorraine Arcudi, stayed with Arrow long enough to gain some responsibility within his operations, have a child, and decide she couldn't stomach his brutish, old world ways," Duggan answered for her. "Before Angelina was born, Lorraine had been given control of prostitution in the name of her husband." Duggan snorted. "He said it was the only thing a woman could handle well."

Angelina herself returned to the table with three plates and some cutlery. Without waiting, she dug into the veal parmigiana.

"After Angelina was born," Duggan continued, "Lorraine had reorganized the business so effectively that when she left him, she took prostitution with her. To show you what kind of man Arrow is, he started a war to get his hookers and wife back."

"Only Momma was a lot stronger than even he suspected," Angelina took over the story. "She had made her own connections. The primary one being Neal here."

Duggan concerned himself with the veal although he could not disguise a wistful smile.

"He helped her build the four houses and he helped defend her when the big guns came in," Angelina went on, putting one arm around the old man's neck.

"I loved her, Mr. Sullivan," Duggan admitted, looking up at him. "I helped her, sure, but she did most of the real work. She had the operation so streamlined and so profitable that the Mob didn't really want it back in Arrow's hands. But it was a matter of masculine pride, so they let the war continue. She fought back. Hard. Finally, the situation became so unbearable that it was brought up at the last Commission meeting in Appalachia in 1957. They decided if Lorraine wanted it that bad and could handle it that well, she should have it. They told Arrow to lay off and mind his own business. The meaning was clear; his business was no longer prostitution."

"That decision stuck until all the *capo di tuttis* died or

100

were killed," said Angelina. "Then he started moving in on her again." She took another bite of veal.

"But he didn't have to kill her, Mr. Sullivan," said Duggan. "Cancer did that for him." Brett saw the old man's eyes misting.

"It wasn't that long ago," Angelina said to Brett although she was looking at Duggan.

"So now he's buried your mother and he's coming after you," Brett summarized.

"That's right," she said earnestly. "Arrow thinks he owns everything he sees and that included my mother and me. He wants it all: cigarettes, linen, prostitution. And he thinks he's strong enough to get it, even against Testi and me at the same time."

"And what do you want?" Brett asked bluntly.

"Just a little peace, Mr. Sullivan. You may have heard me up there. I'm not going to play by my father's rules. I'm not going to scurry around town like a terrorist, killing innocent girls and servants."

"So you know about the Shop," Brett asked.

"Of course," she responded. "As soon as Lenny didn't report in with my share of last night's take, I knew something was wrong."

"Your share?" Brett echoed. "Don't you get it all and divvy out their shares?"

"We don't work that way, Mr. Sullivan. Each of our houses caters to a different and specific clientele. Each manager runs the house the way he or she sees fit. As director I get my cut. I control outside events. They control inside ones. My mother instituted this system and I stick with it."

"It didn't work with the Shop," Brett reminded her. "Why don't you go underground?"

"I take full responsibility for last night's disaster," Angelina flared, "but to run now would be disastrous! Arrow will have won. I promise you, Mr. Sullivan, those

*101*

deaths will not be in vain. The more people my father kills, the worse it will be for him. We have some very powerful and influential clients here. They won't stand for innocent girls being murdered. Especially not their favorite girls."

Brett thought of Cyndi upstairs. He thought about the many people who could get hooked on a girl like that.

"The Shop was our specialty house," Angelina explained further. "If you liked to tie them up or dress them up, you went to the Shop. It was the best establishment of its kind anywhere. I know many law men and judges who are going to be very upset when they find out what happened. I won't have to do anything about my father. The outside world is going to come down on him."

"And what about you, Mr. Sullivan?" interjected Duggan. "What do you want?"

Brett leaned back, closed his eyes for a second and got up. "I just want to make my way in one piece," he drawled. "When the smoke clears, I want to be left standing."

"If you fight the way you did upstairs all the time, I'd give you pretty good odds," Angelina said, laughing.

"It's no laughing matter, Angelina," Duggan stressed, taking her hand in his. "This man was hired to kill you." He looked at Brett intently. "What about that, Mr. Sullivan?"

"I'll do you a favor if you'll do me one," he said. The two seated people continued to stare at him, so he went on. "You put out the word that I got close tonight, but no cigar. Let it be known that I spooked you enough to get you to hide out. Then disappear for a little while." Brett walked to the kitchen door without waiting for an answer. He picked up the duffel he had retrieved from Cyndi's room after giving her a kiss and a big tip.

"And in return?" said Duggan as Brett was halfway out the door.

Shack Sullivan stopped and poked his head back in. "I'll wait a little while," he said. "See who deserves to die. Thanks for the dinner."

"I like your style," said George Arrow the next morning. He was seated in another office, across the hall and to the right of the office he had been in the day before. The only difference between the two places was that next to the curtains and windows behind Arrow's desk was a brick wall. On one side of the hallway was the Atlantic Ocean. On the other side was solid cement. No one was going to assassinate the Mob boss from either direction.

The security for the whole office complex was cunning. The lobby had fake doors as a diversion and the real door could only be opened by a system of four buttons with a combination changed constantly. After that Arrow changed his office every day so he was never pinned down in one room. He was a veteran of Mob wars and he liked staying alive.

"They tell me you almost got Arcudi last night," Arrow went on. "Took out some of their best guards doing it, too. Very impressive for the first time out."

"Bullshit," Brett muttered. "Arcudi got away."

"But you got out alive," Arrow reminded him. "Alive to complete the contract another day."

"I'll get him tonight," Brett vowed. He didn't hit the pronoun "him" with any undue force, and he watched Arrow closely when he said it. The man looked pleased. His little "joke" of sending him to kill a young woman was still a secret as far as he was concerned. Brett's joke on him was that he survived.

"Don't worry about it," Arrow said benevolently. "Arcudi's gone into hiding. I wanted Arcudi out of the way and you accomplished that. Now we have bigger fish to fry."

"Testi?" Brett asked expectantly.

"Easy, Tiger, easy," Arrow chortled. "You'll get your stab at the man himself soon enough." Brett allowed himself to sink back into the chair disappointedly. "First there's a lieutenant of his who's making my life here very difficult. I don't want him just out of the way. I want him out of my life. No, I'll get him next time. Understand?"

"Understood," replied Brett. "Same deal as before?"

The Phoenix hotel-casino construction site was a marvel to behold, especially at night. The crews were working overtime to finish it for its scheduled opening, so the skeleton structure was lit up like a billboard. It had almost as many lights strung across it now as it would when it opened in October. But for now, it was a husk with hundreds of men crawling over it like bees in a hive.

Through its open walls on three sides, Brett could see the other hotels and casinos winking and blinking at the night sky. There was Caesars and Bally backed up on the Boardwalk. The Resorts International between Boardwalk and Park Place. The Penthouse establishment wrapped around the tiny two-story hotel that wouldn't sell out to them. There was the glittering Boardwalk Regency with its shaped cathedral mirrors reflecting everything within eyeshot. There was the regal Resorts International with its El Casino designed with an Arabian Nights flavor. There was the Brighton and Harrah's near the marina.

They were all there and they were all straight. Not one had the taint of organized crime on it. But it was out there and it was growing. Brett turned to look out the other side of the structure. The Atlantic Ocean stretched off into the horizon, oblivious. Brett stopped his reverie and got busy loading bricks.

He was dressed in workman's clothing. He had come to the location at the change of shifts at four-thirty in the afternoon dressed in work shirt and jeans. He grabbed a hat and joined the crew on the lower floors. Behind protective glasses and under the orange safety helmet, no one really noticed him. Temps were coming onto this rush job all the time. In fact, he positioned himself so that managers would send him on rudimentary jobs which kept him active. If he was working, no one would ask him what he was doing there.

So he piled bricks, hauled materials, and just generally thought about his two days stuck in the middle of a Mob war. Everyone he had met so far was testing him. He had proved his worth and expertise all the way around, but in the underworld, no one was to be trusted completely. And the only definite thing you ever did was to die. The commonness of sudden death here was demonstrated by the way both Arrow and his daughter reacted to the deaths of their guards. Soldiers were expendable—that was why they were soldiers.

Brett compared it to the golden days of the samurai in Japan. As members of the warrior class, these men could do anything they wanted with the classes below them. And those classes consisted of anyone not a samurai or shogun adviser. They could legally, if not morally, carry out their every whim on the "commoners" the same way Arrow could test Brett's prowess on his guards. Arrow was a long-standing member of the Italian warrior class. Only they had no code of honor anymore.

There was one other comparison between the Mob and the samurais that Brett could easily make. The underworld in Atlantic City was like the samurai of the 1890s. The Emperor had wrested his power back from his general, the Shogun. Suddenly there was no more need of samurai. When gambling was legalized in Atlantic City, suddenly the Mob's main source of illegal gain was gone. So, like the samurai, they continued to fight. But they did not fight for survival, like the Japanese warrior class. They fought over bed sheets. They fought over towels. They killed for laundry.

A last connection between the old world samurai and the new world Mob. Both had a ninja in their midst to do the dirty work.

Aaron Schonberger arrived at the Phoenix construction site at nine o'clock—well into the night shift. He was the man Arrow had sent Brett after. As he watched the middle-aged Jewish money man walk toward the elevator with his two guards, Brett remembered what the Mob boss had said about him. He was arranging an above-board deal to get Testi involved with the Phoenix. If he succeeded, Testi would have a legitimate, concrete foundation in Atlantic City upon which to build.

Arrow only leased his headquarters in the Diamond Head resort, as Testi leased his in the Gold Rush hotel-casino. At least it looked that way on paper. Their involvement in their respective headquarters went much deeper, but the evidence was too far down for any investigator to find it. But if Testi went in on the Phoenix as a straight businessman, his sphere of influence might spread so far that even Arrow couldn't match or contain him.

If Schonberger were to die, the investors would be scared away and Testi would have a message. That message would read "you take control over my dead body." Arrow made it clear to Shack Sullivan that if he did this job right, the reward for him would be much greater than the final half of twenty-five-thousand dollars. Arrow hinted he'd happily hand over a piece of the action when he got his fingers on all of it.

Arrow had only one instruction to Brett concerning the death of Schonberger. "Make it spectacular," he said.

Brett began to work his way over to the building's ledge. He knew exactly where they'd stop first. The construction manager's office was on the seventh floor. Brett saw no way the innocuous money man would go look at building trouble spots before conferring with the manager, who could then act as tour master. Brett walked to the very edge of the third floor and jumped off. He landed on a beam that was being hauled up by a crane. He rode the metal for three floors and jumped off again. He landed on the seventh floor.

"Hey, hey, hey," he heard a man yell at him. He looked over to see a brawny, red-faced worker carrying some crumpled blueprints stalking toward him. "What the hell do you think you're doing?" the man screamed at Brett over the noise of the machinery.

"Just hitching a ride," Brett answered diffidently.

"Well, we don't go for that kind of bullshit anymore!" the man yelled. "There are unions, you know, hotshot! We got safety rules around here! You could have closed us down for the night if any inspector had seen you! What group are you with, hot dog?"

"Man, I don't know," Brett complained huffily. "I just reported to work tonight. Somebody tells me to do something, I do it, that's all."

The man with the blueprints slapped his free hand to his brow and looked up at the unfinished ceiling. "God save me from local help," Brett heard him say. He grabbed Brett's arm as he looked back down. "Come on, hotshot! You're coming with me to see the construction manager. Maybe he can get this thing straightened out!"

Brett went along willingly as the man pulled him toward the center of the floor. If his little open air jaunt hadn't brought the manager to him as he thought it might, he was just as pleased to go over to the manager. He took very careful note of the construction activity going on around him as he approached the manager's makeshift office next to the open elevator shaft.

Some men to his right were working out room boundaries with metal poles, hammers, automatic screwdrivers, and crowbars. Men off to his left were doing some riveting work on a major column. Men behind him were stockpiling some beams. In front of him was the elevator shaft, composed of metal link walls on three sides and an open front. The elevator was moved by thick wires attached to its ceiling and floor. It was open on two sides.

Brett saw the wires hanging from the ceiling to floor of the seventh story tense, then the roof of the elevator rose into view. The Ninja Master had timed it perfectly. He was going to be at the manager's side at the same moment Schonberger got there.

Usually when Brett was set to kill, an unearthly calm descended upon him. He was not tense or nervous in the least. The talents he had developed reached their zenith of proficiency when he killed. Only now, drawing near the construction manager's office with Schonberger rising into view, he felt a certain irritating chill, as if his entire body had gone to sleep for a second.

A second later it was gone. Brett was in as much control as he could be. He remembered what he had told Jeff Archer about controlling outside events with inner strength, his *ki*. And he knew why he suddenly got the crawling vibration. He was preparing himself *not* to kill with all the skill and prowess he usually drew upon to terminate life. If his plan was to work, he'd need to use all the capabilities that he had.

Aaron Schonberger came into view. He was a medium-looking man in every way. He was middle-aged, of medium height, of medium weight, and of medium temperament. He had a small brow, curling gray-black hair, a gray mustache and thick eyeglasses. He wore a blue double-knit overcoat. The two guards on either side of him were the usual issue. One was young and looked like he practiced being Sylvester Stallone every night in front of the mirror. The other was a hulking, thick-lipped Italian brute of the nature you'd see in redubbed "Son of Hercules" movies.

Brett and his warder reached the manager's front door just as the elevator stopped and the manager himself emerged. The warder tried to yell the story at the man in the long-sleeved shirt with the arms rolled up and the tie loosened, but he turned away from the angry supervisor to help Schonberger out of the elevator. The money man, like the manager, was wearing a special blue safety helmet. The bodyguards were wearing regulation orange ones. The supervisor turned angrily back to Brett as the manager undid the one thin chain from the front of the shaft which served as protection.

"You just wait a second," the supervisor said to Brett with conviction. "This'll be over in a second."

Brett agreed with him silently. He waited until the supervisor began to turn back toward the manager and then he moved.

Both his hands were suddenly on the supervisor's back and he shoved. The man flew forward, ramming into the manager. Both men fell in a jumbled heap onto the floor of the elevator. Schonberger and his guard duo were taken by surprise. They were directly in front of the shaft, looking over their shoulders at the two figures trying to disentangle themselves. When they looked forward to see what had caused the fall, they were practically staring into the placid face of Brett Wallace.

He was racing forward as their eyes settled on him and just as they adjusted their minds to seeing him coming toward them, he sprang up. He rose twelve feet into the air, his hair just grazing the ceiling. The guards' hands moved automatically toward their underarms even as their amazed eyes were following his progress. They never had a chance to reach their guns.

Brett soared forward from that height, going right over Schonberger's head. At the apex of his flight, the edges of his boots snaked out in both directions, crashing into the side of each guard's head. They fell away from Schonberger like a peel from a banana. Brett landed behind the money man and between the unconscious guards. As he spun, he grabbed Schonberger's left arm and wrenched it up behind his back. His other hand gripped the man's neck and started massaging a nerve.

"Just relax," he instructed quickly and quietly, "and you won't be hurt."

Brett propelled the man forward toward the northwest corner of the seventh floor. It would have been frightening for Schonberger to see the floor run out and the yawning air beyond, but instead he felt an ethereal sense of calm brought on by Brett's acupressure. So when Brett hurled him off the edge of the floor and down toward the brown-green ground below, he felt peaceful, like he was flying.

He was so relaxed that he landed on the safety net—erected on each corner of the third floor to catch falling materials and equipment—perfectly. He rolled over lazily in the air and landed flat on his back. He bounced straight up into the air twice, then settled comfortably in the hemp.

Upstairs, the manager and supervisor had scrambled to their feet. As far as they could see, Brett had thrown Schonberger to his death.

"Stop that man!" the manager screamed, pointing wildly at Brett. As he said it, Brett glanced over his shoulder to see a gang of enraged construction workers coming at him with hammers, a riveter, and a crowbar.

The curved end of the crowbar came at his head first from above. He ducked to the left side and hurled his arm back straight from the shoulder. He met the iron rod in midair, his arm settling in the crook just above his elbow. The force of his return swing pushed the bar in another direction and made the swinging worker feel as if he had just hit a petrified redwood tree. The tool was wrenched out of the man's hands. It swung down around Brett's elbow where he grabbed it with his other hand and lifted it off his arm.

The movement didn't stop. It continued so Brett could

parry the incoming jab of the riveting machine, using the crowbar like a sword. The large, vibrating machine was deflected for a second, allowing Brett to snake the curved end of the bar around so that it gripped the riveter handle. With a quick tug, he pulled it out of the worker's hands.

Brett dropped both implements as the surprised worker stumbled forward. He then swung his hands from left to right, throwing the unbalanced man into the remaining two workers with the hammers. The man who had the crowbar was the only guy left standing. He charged Brett with all the anger and strength he had.

The one thing Brett didn't want to do was kill any innocent workers, so he couldn't just dodge and let the man run or trip right off the edge of the floor. The two antagonists collided, Brett pushing himself back against the clutching arms of the worker. They both skidded near the floor edge, then Brett pulled himself down beneath the worker's grip. He then simply placed his elbow securely between the man's legs.

It was quite possibly the lightest blow Brett had ever delivered, but it did the trick. The man doubled over, his face purple, his arms paralyzed. Brett merely stood up, the top of his head colliding with the wounded man's chin. The worker fell flat on his back, mercifully unconscious. Insurance and worker compensation would handle the rest, Brett had no doubt.

But as the man fell away from him, Brett saw another small army of men running forward to take his place. Brett knew he could break through them to get to the elevator, but he wasn't sure whether he could do it without inadvertently killing someone. He glanced over his shoulder quickly. During his initial defense, several men had crawled out to retrieve the fallen Schonberger. Brett saw them taking him back to his limousine, its engine already running.

Brett planted his feet on the very edge of the floor, half

his body hanging over the hard Atlantic City dirt seven stories below. He saw the Central Pier off to the left. It was a huge wooden structure that poked out into the ocean, its length covered with stores and meeting places closed for the night. He saw Schonberger getting ever closer to his car.

Brett leaned over onto the edges of his feet and ran toward the corner of the floor. The attacking workers stopped dead in their tracks when they saw the man who had attacked Schonberger seem to start falling off the building, then float in space. He appeared to be in a perpetual leaning posture—except that he was running!

The edges of Brett's feet snaked in front of each other to move unerringly toward the building's corner. His balance was astonishing, as he meant it to be. The workers were too busy marveling at the living contradiction in natural laws to attack him. Once Brett had reached the corner and was directly over the net which was closest to the revving limo, he let gravity, which had been tugging at him, pull him over. He dove straight down at the net.

At the last possible second, he somersaulted over onto his back, landing flat, and bouncing back up fifteen feet. At the summit of his bounce, Brett brought his body straight and around, so he was falling facing toward the building. Looking down, he saw the six places the net was attached to the building side. He hit the net again, feet first, using it like a trampoline to propel him toward the net connecting points.

As he was flying forward, he was also crouching and turning his hand into the *yohon nukite* position—the spear head. As he landed a second time, his hands lashed forward, cutting the connecting ropes as surely as if his fingers had been blades. This sort of chopping maneuver took all the strength and speed he possessed. Do it even slightly wrong and the fingers would bend or bounce or be deflected away.

The ropes tore across and the net began to fall away. Brett used the crosshatched hemp as a ladder to climb toward the next connecting point even as the prior one was falling away. He was working left to right, so the large net was swinging down, like a sail in the wind, toward Schonberger's car. Brett moved quickly on, climbing the falling net and chopping at the connections.

Finally there were only two left. Brett dove forward, seeing Schonberger get into the back of his limo beneath him. He speared the second to last connection then threw his body back and down. For a second he saw the net fluttering in front of him, then empty air. At that moment he reached up and grabbed the loose end of the netting. His weight and motion turned the net into a rope for him to swing on. It brought him down far enough so he wouldn't break a bone when landing and forward far enough so he was in front of Schonberger's car.

Brett let go of his makeshift "Tarzan" rope. He flew forward and fell twenty feet at the same time. He landed and rolled in the dirt, having to somersault four times to cushion the shock. Then he was up and running at the car which was trying to navigate a U-turn out of the construction site. Brett saw the driver before the chauffeur saw him. The driver was dressed in dark blue with the customary cap. He was seated behind the wheel with his window closed and door locked.

That didn't stop Brett. All the driver knew was that Schonberger had been gently hurried into the back and a workman had told him in no uncertain terms to get him out of here. The driver didn't know why and the money man himself wasn't talking. He just sat in the back with a dazed look on his face. So the chauffeur was taken completely by surprise when a hand came blasting through the window.

The driver saw it in a strange sort of slow-motion close-

113

up. His mind registered a cracking thunder first and his peripheral vision picked up the glass breaking away from the tips of five fingers huddled together. Then the window blew in and the fingers spread out, smacking into the side of the driver's head.

Brett had broken the window with his hand in the devastating *keiko* position—the chicken beak hand. It sounded ludicrous, but with his thumb next to his pinkie and the three main fingers piled on top of those, his hand made up a flesh and blood bullet that seemed capable of plowing through anything. The only reason he spread his fingers is that if he hit the side of the driver's head in the *keiko* position, he would have killed him for sure. It was vitally important that he stay in Schonberger's good graces. And that meant he not kill someone the money man might like.

As it was, the chauffeur fell across the front seat, almost knocked out. The car kept barreling forward as Brett held on and searched for the lock. He finally found the correct switch, jabbed it and threw open the door. He grabbed the side and top of the opening and pulled himself in.

He tried to sit down as the groggy driver was kicking out by instinct and rolling around the seat. "I'll kill you," the brutish man said, trying to drag himself into a sitting position. "I'll kill you," he repeated to no one in particular. He hadn't identified his assailant yet. All he wanted was to sit up and see the man who had attacked the car. All Brett wanted to do was stop him.

The car was still moving and the door was still open when Brett grabbed the chauffeur and started dragging him out. The driver was kicking and jerking in the small enclosed area of the front seat, making it very difficult for Brett to get a grip. In the claustrophobic enclosure filled with swinging limbs, all the Ninja Master could count on was his strength. Doing martial arts moves against a nearly unconscious man in the front seat of a limo would be ridiculous as well as dangerous.

Getting his butt flat on the driver's seat, Brett wrenched both of the chauffeur's kicking legs over his lap, grabbed a handful of the man's shirt front and pushed him up. The man's head slammed on the ceiling of the car, pushing his hat over his eyes. With him sitting up, Brett could see the gun in his shoulder holster under his loose coat and the hand that was reaching for it.

"I'll kill you," the driver continued to babble. "I swear I'll kill you."

Brett grabbed his wrist as his hand clamped on the weapon. Brett tightened his grip on the driver's wrist and helped him pull the gun out. It was the infamous snub-nose revolver with the taped handle. It was the favorite weapon of Mob killers everywhere. Brett wrapped his free fingers around the gun's chamber so it wouldn't move even if the chauffeur tried to pull the trigger. At the same time, the driver rediscovered the use of his own free hand, swung it up and tried to claw at whatever he could find of Brett.

The two figures struggled on the front seat as the car continued to travel. Brett moved his head away from the driver's hooked fingers, winding up looking out the front windshield. He saw that they were speeding to the left of the construction entrance—heading right toward the chain-link fence. That inspired him to finish the fight. As the large, sleek car plowed into the metal, ripping the mooring links right out of the ground and sending a sharp ended section of metal points ripping across the paint job with a sound of uncoiling springs, Brett tore the revolver out of the driver's hand and threw the man across his lap.

The chauffeur dropped out of the car, rolled across the sidewalk and dropped into the street as Brett spun the wheel to the left. He wasn't fast enough to prevent the car careening into a parked vehicle across the street from the construction site, pushing in the parked car's doors and ripping the limo's headlights off. But he was fast enough to keep the car going. He redirected it down the street and took a hard, screeching left onto the Central Pier, leaving two hubcaps behind. As the big, crumpled car disappeared behind the pier's stores, the hubcaps rolled crazily back down the street.

The stunned workmen on the unfinished Phoenix watched as the limo barreled down the pier, appearing between the stores and disappearing again behind another building. They looked to the dock's end, where it dropped off thirty feet to the water. They looked back to see the car pass by the last store at full speed.

Incredibly the vehicle exploded before it had even left the pier. Suddenly, for seemingly no reason, the car erupted with a huge ball of flame, tearing the roof off and scattering all the windows in a large, glittering circle. The blast pushed the car down on its tortured shocks and wheels for a second, but it didn't stop it. The flaming mass of metal rammed the pylons at the end of the pier, smashed them aside, and vaulted into the air.

The slab of flying fire dove twenty feet forward, its destroyed tires still spinning, and thirty feet down to belly-flop into the water. A huge circular wave went up and out, but it failed to quench the flames. Even after the car quickly sank, the fire remained, broiling on the surface of the sea.

The workmen raced each other to get off the hotel structure and run the length of the street and pier. A large crowd of them gathered at the dock's end, looking down into the hissing mass of burning oil. No one harbored any thoughts of a heroic rescue try.

Brett Wallace watched the construction crew from the safety of one of the stores. He had broken in after dragging Schonberger out of the still moving car. He turned away from the sight, moving over to where the still groggy Schonberger sat, the smoking, empty revolver lying next to his legs.

"Sorry, my friend," Brett said quietly. "But you had to die. Spectacularly, with witnesses."

# Chapter Five

The Gold Rush hotel-casino was at the peak of its midnight business. The huge casino was awash with people of all kinds. There were men in shirtsleeves and tuxedos. There were women in dresses and pantsuits. There were men and women wearing most everything in between as well. They were of many ages and all sizes. Brett even saw a midget standing on a chair to work the slot machines.

The walls were done in a brownish red motif to complement the green felt of the tables. There were dark, shiny columns placed intermittently across the floor. The rug could hardly be glimpsed amid the thousands of shoes. The ceiling was mirrored with half-globes stuck every few feet. The globes seemed to stare down at the roulette, blackjack, baccarat, craps and big six tables. The entire place was orchestrated, jostling movement.

Aaron Schonberger led Brett through the throng toward the far wall. Installed there were permanent booths for money changers and cashiers. Schonberger went right up and was let right in. He vouched for Brett, who followed. They moved down along the back wall as men and women paid out and listened to stories of triumph, tragedy, and indifference. Brett saw almost every kind of forced expression possible on the faces of the gamblers he passed.

Finally they came to a red, padded door in the very corner of the last cashier's location. There was a circle of small black buttons above the knob which Schonberger hit in a special sequence. Only then did he pull out a key from his vest's watch pocket and insert it in the lock. The key was attached to a watch chain. The money man put the key and chain back in place before turning the knob and pulling the door open. He went in first, Brett following.

They entered a plain, empty room consisting of four concrete walls. The only break in the beige blocks was a flat, gray plate nestled seven feet above the floor and the knobless iron door below it.

"Come on," said Schonberger irritably. "Open up. He's safe."

The iron door slid to the left. Aaron led the way again as Brett smiled with thanks at the gray plate. He had no doubt that a camera was behind it. They walked a long, plain hallway lined with doors, took a right at the end, and walked down another length of floor. They took a final turn to the right into a brightly lit office consisting of one desk, three chairs, and a standing man.

"Go on in," the man said, motioning to a plain door between the desk and the chairs. Schonberger went over and opened this door with no problem. Brett assumed that most of the security devices were now behind them.

Inside was a large office space, richly carpeted with

beige shag. The walls were completely covered with floor-to-ceiling curtains, making Brett wonder what was behind them besides wall. Against the right-hand curtains was a huge video console lined with screens picturing various Gold Rush locations. To the left was a circle of sofas and seats which were used for meetings, no doubt. And between those two sections was a gigantic desk made up of a thick shellacked slice from the trunk of a redwood tree and four smaller tree stumps which served as legs.

Behind this huge desk was a man worthy of it. He was tall, muscular, and brown-haired. His face was wide and strong with sharp blue eyes set over a thin, long nose and wide lips. There were groups of lines at the corners of the lips and eyes. The man was dressed in a tan leisure suit and expensive athletic shoes. This man was unmistakably John Testi. Everything about his manner and posture said that he was the boss. But unlike Arrow, he looked like a man one could follow without being forced to.

He didn't play any games. As soon as Schonberger and Brett had placed themselves in front of the massive desk, the Atlantic City Mob leader leaned forward and spoke to his money man. "So this is the man who killed you and then brought you back from the dead?" Schonberger had set the meeting up by phone, so the basic facts were already established.

"That's right, Mr. Testi," Schonberger replied in that assistant vice-principal tone of voice he had. His tone held only a certain amount of authority that way. Testi was obviously the entire school board in the money man's mind. "Shack Sullivan," Schonberger introduced, pivoting between Brett and the man behind the tree trunks. "John Testi." Neither man held out his hand. Testi kept them below the lip of his desk and Brett kept them at his sides. They acknowledged each other with small nods.

"Aaron tells me you got him safely off a seven-story building and out of a speeding car," Testi told Brett

120

calmly. "None of it sounds easy or even particularly pleasant. How did you manage to do it?"

"I learned a few things along the way," Brett replied, going through his Shack Sullivan story again for Testi's benefit. "When I got onto the pier and was heading straight for the water," he finished up, "I jumped into the back seat, made sure Schonberger was still limp, got us both out, then kept shooting at the car until I hit the gas tank. Then, when the construction workers approached, I got Schonberger out of sight."

Brett hadn't told the truth about his name, his past, and the gas tank. He hadn't just shot aimlessly at the gas tank. With incredible preciseness and purpose, he pumped each of the .38-caliber rounds into the exact same spot until they dug their way into the tank. One bullet alone did not have the power to break through all that metal. But one bullet pushing the next did the trick. The ninja had a name for that skill. *Hojutsu,* the art of firearms.

"Very impressive," Testi responded to Brett's story. "You went through a lot of trouble to make it appear as if Aaron was killed." Testi became thoughtful and pursed his lips. "The question now is why?"

"I thought that would be obvious," Brett came back reasonably. "I don't like the side I'm fighting on. I don't like the odds. Everything could be easy here. There's enough cash flow around town to keep everybody happy, but Arrow's getting vindictive. He's sending me out to kill women and economists. It's not good business."

"Women?" Testi echoed, straightening up in his seat.

"Yeah," Brett retorted. "You heard about the Shop slaughter by now, haven't you?"

Testi relaxed again. "Yes," he concurred. "I've heard about it. I've also heard some other things. Things about a newcomer named Shack Sullivan who only arrived a few days ago but has been coming on strong. I heard about him saving Arrow from a hit man. A hit man I

121

didn't hire. Then I hear he's Arrow's new hired dog. Then all of a sudden he's in my office, making nice noises."

Suddenly Testi brought his arms up from under his desk. His left arm was fine, the hand strong, the fingers long. The right arm was nonexistent. In its place was a hunk of metal ending in a hydraulic hook. Testi slammed his steel forearm down on the desk. It made an echoing, thumping sound.

"You strike me as a very undependable type of guy, Mr. Sullivan," Testi said ominously.

"Not undependable, Mr. Testi," Brett said immediately without blinking an eye. "Undecided. A good sailor doesn't go out to sea without checking to see which way the wind is blowing, does he? A guy could drown that way." The whole time he was speaking, he was checking out Testi's artificial limb. On second glance, it looked as if Testi had organic material to his elbow and the metal went on from there. The hook was made by one thick wire bent double, shaped and sharpened at the hook point. Another single wire was shaped and installed between the bent hook to serve as a metal thumb. It was moored in a round stump which disappeared up Testi's sleeve.

"A good sailor also doesn't take on a job he has no intention of fulfilling," Testi answered Brett's metaphor. "A guy could die that way just as easily."

"No," said Brett flatly. "Not just as easily. A sailor is only as good as his ship. If one is sinking, you can't blame him for getting another. Only the captain has to go down with the ship."

Testi considered the point, leaning back and closing his eyes. "Touché," he said, opening his eyes and pulling his metal arm off the table. "You're correct, Mr. Sullivan. In this business, it makes good sense to test the waters and moor your boat to a solid rock. I take it, then, by Aaron's ongoing health, that you made your decision as to which captain you'll serve under?"

"I'm just hired help, Mr. Testi," Brett said humbly, sitting down in a chair to the left of the desk. "I was paid to get Arcudi out of the way. I got Arcudi out of the way. I was paid to get rid of Schonberger. As far as Arrow knows, Schonberger is gone. One thing I haven't been paid for is to get rid of John Testi. It seems to me a good idea would be to pay for Arrow's death first. Then I'm obligated."

Testi chuckled. "You're top class, I'll give you that," he said, rising from his seat and holding onto his metal forearm. "You come roaring into town and in the space of twenty-four hours prove yourself to be somebody everybody wants. You got no past and you're living your present in the fast lane." Testi slowly worked his way around the desk as his real hand worked its way down to his hook.

As he grew near Brett, he suddenly twisted the hook to the right. It popped right out of its base. In its place was a thin, two-edged stiletto which sprang out from inside the stump. In a second, the blade was at Brett's throat.

"You've got to be extra careful if you want to have any future at all," Testi advised him quietly. Then the knife was pulled away and Testi returned to his seat. When he faced Brett and Schonberger again, the knife was gone and the hook was back in place.

"All right," he agreed. "You know Arrow, and you can get to him because he trusts you. I'll let you kill him. I'll pay you any price you suggest to get the job done. I won't quibble. Anything to get this war over with so things can get back to normal around here."

It took just a few minutes to work out the details. Testi would pay one hundred thousand dollars to see that Arrow died; fifty thousand up front and fifty thousand afterward. Brett gave him the name and number of a bank account he took out just for the purpose of stashing away the hit money. Testi could transfer the sum directly into the account so Brett did not have to carry the sum around with him. Testi sent Schonberger right off to set it up.

"Poor guy," Testi clucked after the money man left. "He's brilliant but not very smart. If he had any failings at all, it would be his loyalty. He likes me and thinks friendship should extend to working like this. What a guy. As far as he's concerned, you saved his life. He doesn't even remember that you came to end it."

Testi saw Brett to the knobless iron door of the cement room between the office complex and the cashiers' booths himself. He wished him the best of luck and warned him not to change sides again. "Once we're crossed, there's no coming back," he said. "You'll be out in the middle of two warring mobs. And nobody, not even you, can get out of something like that alive."

Brett nodded and went into the cement room. Testi closed the door behind him. They hadn't shaken hands. Brett walked toward the opposite door. Halfway there, the sound of a thunderclap suddenly filled the room. After that, there was no air left to breathe. In the space of a second, the tiny cell had become a vacuum.

For the first time since returning from the Orient, Brett was taken completely by surprise. The trap nearly overwhelmed him in its deadly simplicity. And there was nothing he could do. His initial response was shocked paralysis. His mind screamed at him to do something, but the sound of his brain cry drifted away at the end. He had only his basic instinct and two seconds of consciousness left.

His chest felt filled with steel wool. His throat felt like a solid iron bar. His hypersensitivity made him feel his eyes bulging, tongue hanging out and the tiny sound of blood vessels bursting everywhere. He lunged forward, his hand in the *keiko* position. But surprise threw his style off. His fingers slammed into the second door just a few millimeters off. There wasn't enough strength behind the blow to even chip the fortified concrete covering. Brett slammed down, pain lancing up his fingers toward a brain that was already going dead.

The wind roared through his head as he lay crumpled against the wall. And suddenly he realized that it was not the sound of eternity wailing, but the sound of air being pumped back into the room. Slowly, painfully, Brett sat up, discovering that sweat covered his entire body and he had been drooling. He pushed himself up and around so that he sat with his back to the second door.

Looking up, he saw John Testi standing in the open doorway to the offices. His expression could only be called one of superiority. "You're not playing with dumb African savages now, Sullivan," he said evenly. "That's just as simple as it is. One second you're fine. The next second you're dead. Remember that."

Testi turned to walk away, but just before he made it all the way around, he stopped and looked at Brett again. "Oh," he added absentmindedly, "if you're harboring any thoughts about fulfilling your contract on Angelina, forget about it. She's mine."

It was several minutes before Brett could make his body breathe normally. It, like almost anyone else in that situation, wanted to gulp in the air like a man in the desert going after water. It was an especially shocking blow to his body given that his training hadn't seen a single clue, threat, or warning that it was going to happen. If Testi hadn't been teaching him a lesson, the Ninja Master would have been dead by now.

Brett vowed that it would be a lesson well learned. He moved around the city until he was sure he wasn't being followed, then he moved around the city some more until he was positive. Only then did he go over to the Shop. The little house was empty and a "For Sale" sign was posted in the front yard. It was almost two o'clock at night, so the neighborhood was quiet and dark. The only sounds were the birds, the insects and the far-off sounds of Boardwalk revelry. Even though the Victorian house was fairly far from where the casino action was, it was only a few blocks from Boardwalk, which traversed the length of the city.

Brett purposely climbed up the side of the house and slipped into the attic. Once there, he fell to his knees and threw up. The total weight of what happened dropped on him like a wrecked building. He had taken the Atlantic City reconnaissance like some sort of dojo exercise where he jumped in and out of the pan into the fire, thinking he'd never get burned. But now he was playing both sides of the fence with two men who didn't think twice about murder and had the expertise and money to kill anyway, anyhow. He would never underestimate them again.

Brett cleared his head and rose to his feet. He forgot about his near death. He forgot about his sudden sickness. All he wanted to do was concentrate on the situation and correct it. If he succeeded in killing both Testi and Arrow, there would always be someone to take their places. And even the Ninja Master couldn't destroy the entire Mob without taking most of the country with it.

No, he had to facilitate a singular solution to the specific Atlantic City problem. He had to choose the lesser of two evils. Kill Testi, and Arrow would continue to wage war until he had everything in his pocket. Kill Arrow, and Testi would remain to pick up the pieces. Testi, however, had never waged war on Arcudi. But what did he mean by Angelina being his?

Brett remembered what the girl had said about her mother. She had made a lot of powerful contacts. She had "connections" of her own. The word "connect" in Mafia lingo was the meaning of the Mob itself. They never referred to their organization as the Cosa Nostra or anything else. When any words were needed, they simply said "he's connected." Could one of Lorraine's connections have been John Testi?

Brett shook all the questions out of his mind. He had to deal with practical reality only. As far as Testi knew, he was who he said he was: Shack Sullivan, hired assassin. There was no possible way for him to know of Brett Wallace even if he had suspicions. So the fact was that Testi told Sullivan to lay off the outside hits. He told him not to kill Arcudi. As far as Brett wanted to know, that meant that Testi was sincere. He wanted things peaceful. He'd handle his piece and let Angelina alone.

His conclusion wasn't completely satisfying, but Brett ignored the annoying little buzz in the back of his mind and went downstairs. He entered Vicki Kelly's old room. Everything was gone now except for the curtain liners hanging above the window. They fluttered forlornly in the slight breeze created by a hole in the window.

Brett stood where her bed used to be and where he had found her tortured corpse. He acknowledged that he couldn't be everywhere and he didn't know everything.

But murder was everywhere. Vicki could have been anyone else, he admitted to himself. Someone's wife, or a single girl raped by the psycho next door. Or a rich old lady murdered by a burglar for her jewels. Or a little girl by a gang. Or anybody. He knew, even as he was thinking about it, that someone was getting murdered every second. And there was nothing he could do about it. He could not be everywhere. Even Brett's own whole family had been raped, tortured, and murdered in just forty minutes while he was away.

Brett's entire body moved. It seemed to flow upwards from his legs, which were positioned in a perfect *zenkutsu dachi* karate stance. The force flowed through the center of his being and was channeled across his shoulders and back. His fist leaped forward, propelled by the force of his entire soul. His mouth opened wide and the *kiai* cry that emerged actually shattered the broken bedroom window and vibrated through the entire house.

Brett heard the echo of his incredible shout as he came back to reality. He had blacked out for a minute, not knowing where he was or what he was doing. He looked forward to see his arm buried in the bedroom wall up to his pectoral muscle. Suddenly he felt the night breeze on his fist. He pulled back. His arm came easily out of a crumbling hole in the wall. He had punched completely through the plaster and siding to the outside.

Brett looked at his arm and hand. They were unscratched. Except for some plaster dust covering his knuckles and sleeve, he was completely unscathed. He remembered his own words suddenly: "Only compete against yourself. Your will can be sapped otherwise." Brett had been pitting Shack Sullivan against George Arrow and John Testi. There were no winners in that group.

Brett raced back upstairs, tearing off his clothes as he went. Stamping into the attic, he went to the section of ceiling he had worked on after killing Flanaghan. Pulling away some loose boards, he reached in. With one hand he held the *shinobi shozoko,* the uniform of the ninja. With the other he pulled out his jet black *katana* and *wakizashi,* and the samurai swords.

It was time to relegate Shack Sulliven back to the limbo where he came from. That mercenary would win no battles for Brett. He would be needed for just one more bit of communication before he would be gone forever. Then the Ninja Master would take over.

Brett looked down at the dark shirt, pants, boots and hood. He looked at the two long-hilted swords with the slightly curved blades. He remembered a time when it was easier for the ninja. He would be hired to do a job, then complete it or die. There was no real detective work involved other than finding the best way to kill. There was

128

no question of good and evil. He would kill whoever he was told to kill.

Brett forced himself to forget the past, far and near. He had made his decision. With Arrow gone there would be no more war, no more innocent deaths, and no more problem. He'd leave Atlantic City—the legal and corrupt —to carry on with no more interference. But first Brett Wallace had to succeed where about forty years worth of Mob men had failed. He had to kill George Arrow.

"I said put me through to Arrow! I told you before, this is Shack Sullivan, he'll want to talk to me. What do you think I am, crazy? This is a pay phone, for God's sake! I know what I'm doing. Just tell him its me, okay?" Brett looked out the window of the phone booth. In the distance, up in the sky, he saw the crown of the Diamond Head. Not surprisingly, it was shaped like a giant cut diamond with a huge sign that twinkled like one, even in the midmorning sun.

"Hey, kid!" came the jubilant voice of Arrow over the phone receiver. "You're beautiful! I heard what happened last night. You blew up the whole damn car and dumped it in the ocean! That's just beautiful! That's just great! Testi ain't going in on no new casino, that's for sure!"

"You wanted the job done right," Brett replied. "I did it." Then to quell a mental irritation, he asked, "Now what about Arcudi?"

"Forget Arcudi!" Arrow said expansively. "Arcudi isn't a problem anymore. But don't worry. I'm so pleased, you'll get your money for both Arcudi and Schonberger!"

"All right then, we've got to meet," said Brett. "We've got to talk about Testi."

"Yeah," Arrow mused. "Testi. You're right, kid. You earned a shot at the title. Tell you what. I'm having a meeting tonight of my best people. We're all meeting on the bumper-car platform at the Million Dollar Pier at ten o'clock tonight. From there, we'll catch a boat out to my yacht, okay? I want these guys to meet you. You'll be seeing a lot of each other in the future."

"Fine with me," said Brett. They finished up with some inconsequential remarks. It was fine with Brett, all right. In one meeting and with one fell swoop, the Ninja Master could eradicate the core of Arrow's organization. Then all that would be left was a bunch of soldier chickens with their heads cut off. Testi could either get rid of them or pull them into his own outfit.

Brett left the phone booth with his duffel bag under his arm. In it were the tools of his trade. Beneath his khaki shirt and jeans were the main pieces of the *shinobi shozoko*. He felt rested and ready for the mop-up work tonight. He had twelve hours to mentally prepare himself for the vengeance he would exact at ten o'clock that night. He thought about saying good-bye to Angelina and Cyndi and telling them that it was going to be fine, but he eliminated that thought as fast as he had conceived it.

He would get the job done and get out. Then he would leave Atlantic City to its lesser form of evil.

# Chapter Six

The Million Dollar Pier at nine o'clock was a mass of shadows and threatening shapes: broken signs promising the thrill of a lifetime, cut-out clowns with their paint chipping; garbage, moved by the ocean breezes, strewing the walkways. Behind it glittered the new Atlantic City of fast money thrills. In front of it was the solemn, deep sea. The pier had become a monument to the resort which sought to entertain its visitors in another, more innocent way. It was a porthole through which one walked to glimpse the joys of yesterday to get to where the action was today.

Brett felt something strange as soon as he had stepped onto the structure. It was a cloying energy—the taunting spirit of pier memories—as if the barkers, clowns, strippers, and ride runners' consciousnesses remained, daring him to spend that extra dime to win a Kewpie doll or see the bearded lady. Brett felt it under his feet, in the air around his head, and over in the shadows.

There were plenty of shadows to spare. The evening cast a black shroud on the once glamorous pier. What light drifted over from the casinos was swallowed up by the jagged walls and looming roofs of the closed amusements. Only tiny pockets of dim color remained, peeking through the boarded-up merry-go-round, coloring the edges of the small Ferris wheel, and dotting the open, empty shooting galleries.

Brett moved past these ancient attractions toward the bumper car arena near the end of the pier. He felt it was early enough for a reconnaissance but not late enough for anyone to show up before him. Even if some enterprising Arrow associate had come to the prearranged spot an hour early, Brett had taken pains not to be seen. He was dressed in his all-black ninja uniform and was keeping carefully in the shadows. What little skin showed through his hood slit was blackened. The swords he had in his waist sash and the special holder on his back were coal black. Even the special extra weapons on his belt were housed in a black pouch. He was part of the night.

Brett was exhilarated to be back in purposeful action once more. All the investigating he had done before was like walking on thin ice with eggs strapped to your heels. It was good to be back doing specifically what he had been trained to do: moving in silently, killing, and then leaving again unseen and unknown. As he heard the sounds of the Atlantic waves hitting the pier's pilings below, the supernatural calmness he almost always felt before killing washed over him. It was the feeling of perfect oneness that came with the knowledge that what he was doing was right and perfect.

But as he approached the bumper-car facilities, that calm was interrupted. Not shattered, but thrown off by quaking feelings in the pit of his stomach. It was like a sixth sense that shoved his equilibrium off center. It told him that all was not right within his world. Something did not fit in.

Brett looked up to the night sky. Dark clouds masked the moon and starlight, deepening the darkness on the wharf. The first, lonely raindrop fell across the bridge of Brett's nose. More followed as Brett looked back toward the bumper car building. It was a large rectangular structure with open sides. Along the left hand wall was the platform—interrupted by metal railings to keep the crowds in line. The crowds were long gone, so these railings were rusted and bent. On the right, filling most of the building, was the bumper car floor. It was dull but unmistakably metal. Above it was the cross-hatched metal netting that carried the electrical current to the trolleys of the cars.

Only a few cars remained on the large floor. They looked like large beetles with long, straight tails. Only these metal bugs were dead husks. The rain was coming down hard and regularly as Brett grew nearer and tried to identify his disquiet.

He had to attribute it to the lack of a complete solution in this case. Before, he had always been able to eradicate the total evil on every mission. The corrupters and killers had been totally destroyed. But here he knew that only a small problem within the whole could be corrected. He was only chopping off a cancerous growth on a growing monster. He told himself that it was the lack of a total solution which was disturbing his soul. Somehow that didn't do much good.

Brett shook off the uncomfortable feeling and set foot on the bumper-car platform. He felt an immediate sensation he couldn't identify. It was a tingle, a vibration, which emanated from the wood beneath his feet and traveled up his body. He walked forward, trying to localize and define the feeling. As he made each successive step, the vibrations grew stronger, as if the pier's dead spirits were trying to possess him.

Brett Wallace finally understood what was happening one second before it did. That second saved his life. The energy that his feet picked up was just that—energy. Electrical energy that was coursing through active wires beneath the platform which ran throughout the park. His sixth sense picked up the energy, so he felt the surge a microsecond before all hell broke loose.

In the space between the night darkness and the moment the lights went on, Brett threw himself to the ground. As all the building's lights burst into use, he turned from a standing shadow to a black blur caught in a giant spotlight. The blur dissipated to an inky pool on the floor as the night erupted with gunfire. The bumper-car building shook with the sound and fury of chattering automatic weapons and blasting handguns. More crackling light was created by the lead whining off the rusted metal of the bumper-car netting, floor, and railing.

The initial blast failed to locate the Ninja Master, who was flattened against the floor to escape death. In the instant of illumination, Brett's brain finally put it all together. His much maligned senses had been correct all along. It was only the sickness of his soul that prevented him from hearing it correctly. He hadn't felt spirits on the pier, he had sensed the presence of other assassins lying in wait for him. The strange feelings were not attributable to his psychological unrest; they were caused by all his instincts telling him that the meeting was a trap. Only he would not listen. He was so intent upon killing Arrow and leaving the place that he nearly got himself killed.

There was still a very good chance that the Mob men would succeed. Once he understood his position, he sought to do something about it. His first objective was to deprive the gunmen of a target. His mind assimilated the fact that

134

there were killers all around him on every side of the building. There were two shooting from the far side through the open walls. There were two more on either side of the building. And there were two directly behind him on the other side of the rails.

The latter pair would be the first to get a decent bead on him because they were the closest. So Brett rolled toward them—between the poles holding up the railings. The gunmen vainly tried to readjust their aim. Even in the bright light, it was like trying to hit a rolling cloud of black smoke. It seemed to change shape every second. Their bullets would either flash overhead, dig into the wood on every side or pass right through the billowing shape.

Suddenly Brett was off the platform with his feet on the ground. He was directly between the two men stationed at the back wall. He was standing with his profile to both of them, but all they saw was their target almost within point-blank range. Brett spotted the two men's gun hands. He stood in view of all the killers for a second, taking a desperate gamble. He hoped the men on the other side of the bumper-car floor would not shoot because they were afraid of hitting their partners. And he hoped that the two men—who stood but a mere ten feet from him on either side—would shoot because he looked like a sitting duck.

He was right on all counts. Through his incredibly adaptable vision, he saw both men's guns come up at the same time and their trigger-finger muscles tighten.

There is a moment right after the mind instructs the muscles when that order can be rescinded. There is a second after that when the action cannot be stopped. The next moment the action will happen. The space between the second and third step is infinitesimally small. Brett managed to capture that moment, however, as he pulled his body downwards. Even the way he dropped seemed to demand that the Mob men pull their triggers without altering their aim. The two men shot each other, their bullets just missing the top of Brett's head.

The Ninja Master was already moving as the men were falling. He was scuttling quickly over to his right, moving at top speed sideways. As he went, his left hand went for the sword hilt on his back while his right went for the pouch on his belt. For, over the bursts of the two men's guns, Brett had heard the running feet of the two pairs of men on the sides of the building.

All four were headed his way to back up their associates. Brett raced toward the corner where he judged the first man would appear. He was correct. The sound of the man's feet had told Brett that he was the fastest and closest. He came around the corner with his gun in position, and his face set in an expression that indicated he expected Brett to be dead already.

Instead, it was he who died. Utilizing the art of *iaijutsu*, which enabled the ninja to pull their swords out of their scabbards at lightning speed, Brett sent his short blade right through the first man's neck as his right hand came up with two *shuriken*. His next attack would succeed only if his hearing and control of all five fingers on his right hand were perfect.

He only heard the sound of the first man's head coming off and the fountain of blood gouting out of the neck after it. He saw the two other men at the opposite wall coming around the corner. Over the blood and the thump of the first man's head hitting the ground, he heard the man behind the beheaded one bump into the corpse.

Brett pulled the *wakizashi* down and flipped it so that its blade was pointing behind him at about the level of his chest. Then he pivoted so his side pointed at the men down at the other corner. He was positioned so that he looked ready to throw a Frisbee at the duo of killers down the way. Only he threw the two *shuriken* in the same way he would've thrown the plastic disk.

At the same time he moved sideways and backward. The second man came around the nearest corner, stumbling to avoid the falling corpse without a head. His outstretched arms went on either side of Brett's body as he unknowingly ran into the samurai blade.

The *shuriken* sliced through the air toward the two other men. They were standing over their fallen comrade in such a way that the second man was almost blocked by the first. Only his neck and head was visible over the first man's shoulder. Even in the light the *shuriken* were moving so fast that they did not reflect the light back into the killers' eyes until it was too late. They only heard the sound of the metal stars whipping through the air an instant before they struck.

Just before it seemed both whirring weapons would plunge into the first man, the second *shuriken* peeled off from the first, predirected by a slight move of Brett's fourth finger. It curved around the first man's head to center on the second. For all practical purposes, they both hit at the same time. The first arched up to sink into the first man's throat, tearing upward into his head. The second was pushed into a vertical position by the air currents so that one of its points sunk into the second man's eye. Since both blades were covered in a poison of Brett's own devising, it hardly mattered where they landed.

Brett stood motionless for a moment. He felt the weight of the already dead man against his back. He had felt him run onto the *wakizashi* blade all the way up to the hilt. He had felt the man's realization of the shock and pain. Then he had felt the life quickly leave him. But he also felt the all-encompassing calm which had eluded him before. He felt the calm that told him that he was at the height of his powers and that everything was working at peak. It was a sharp, deadly nirvana which told him that the killing was not over yet.

He saw the man's arms on either side of him stiffen, clench, vibrate, and droop. He felt him grow lax and heavier. But he did not pull out the blade that was keeping him upright. He kept it there because he heard the last two of the nearby killers running in his direction from the back wall. He heard them come around the far corner on his side so all they saw was a slumped figure with his back to them. Seeing all the blood on the ground, they assumed this lone standing figure had to be their target. They raised their guns and shot it.

Brett felt the .38-caliber bullets thunk into the dead man from the other side. He spun, careful to stay completely behind the corpse. He knew that while the person could be termed dead, the mind still functioned on automatic for a few seconds. So knowing, Brett kept one hand firm on the sword hilt holding the corpse upright and grabbed the body's gun arm with his other.

The man's Smith & Wesson .38 Special Airweight was perfect. It was light enough to stay in the dead fingers when Brett wrenched the arm backward. The cartilage was ripped apart and the arm bone left the corpse's shoulder socket as it was bent back and up at an unnatural angle. It looked like a man pointing forward with a straight arm, only he was actually pointing back.

Maintaining an acupressure tension, Brett made sure the fingers stayed tight around the gun butt. Then he touched the muscle up on the arm which automatically tightened the trigger finger. The gun blasted twice. Both approaching killers fell backward, lead missiles halfway through their chests.

As they fell back in the rain, Brett's mind spelled it out for him. It had been a trap. They couldn't have seen him, so somehow the lights must've been rigged to turn on when he had stepped on a certain section of the platform. He may have felt the floor section give at the same second he felt the electrical energy surge. It made little difference now. His body had reacted even before he was aware of it.

Brett pulled his short sword quickly from the dead, broken body. It fell back into the mud at Brett's feet. The Ninja Master swung the *wakizashi* down once, quickly, in the rain to wash the blood off. Then it was back in its scabbard in one smooth motion. He stood listening to the night among eight fallen men. Above the cascading thunder of the rain he could pick up a hum. That's all it was—a distant hum—but somehow it burned and festered in his mind. It was out of place.

It was not the hum of the still bright spotlighting of the bumper-car building. It was not the rhythmic roll of the surf against the pilings below. It was coming from above and to the north. The sound was coming from the next pier down, Central Pier. And it was coming closer.

Brett ran further to the right, toward a closed down roller-rink building which was blocking his view. With a tremendous leap, he shot up about one story in height. He grabbed onto a window ledge there and kept his feet running. He quickly climbed up the remaining story on all fours. He pulled himself to the building's roof just as a helicopter spotlight went on.

Through the most damnable of coincidences, he was caught in the circle of light. He threw himself back just as the Wilkinson "Terry" carbine started blasting 9mm rounds into the rink's roof.

Brett fell toward the ground, watching the helicopter's progress all the while. Just before his view was blocked by the roof's lip, he saw a man next to the pilot holding the light, small automatic weapon in his hands. Arrow was no fool. He had set up backup men for the main team of assassins. And he had set them up on a wharf almost a half-mile away.

In addition to the very powerful semiautomatic weapon, the helicopter had a searchlight controlled by the pilot and both men had high-powered binoculars around their necks. They were absurd lengths to go to for a lone hit man, which worried Brett even more. Somehow, not only did Arrow seem to know about "Shack Sullivan's" double cross, he also seemed to know that Sullivan was much more than a simple mercenary.

Brett spun backwards in midair, twisting his body so that he landed on his feet facing the bumper-car building. He hit the ground, somersaulted and came up running toward the nearest corpse. Before his legs had stopped running, he had stripped the nearest body of its jacket and tied up the sleeves. Then he grabbed the dead man and threw him over the side railing onto the metal bumper-car floor. Using the man's belt and tie, he lashed him to a supporting pole in the middle of the floor—the belt under his arms, the tie around his neck.

Then he vaulted back over the side railings to retrieve the jacket, which had since filled up with some water—enough to make a small pool around the tied corpse's feet. Ripping off the dead man's shoes, Brett used the socks to tie his *katana* sword to the dead man's hands. He then raced over to one of the remaining bumper cars nearby. Hopping in, he waited for the helicopter to make its appearance overhead.

Judging only by sound, Brett carefully examined the makeshift fuse for his diversion. The dead man's bare feet were in a puddle of water on the metal floor. His hands were bound to the long metal blade of a samurai sword. Above him was the metal grating of the bumper-car power source. Brett's first clue was that the spotlights which initially went on seemed part of the building—not specifically attached to catch Brett. So if they were on, that implied power for the entire structure was on. Brett shook the rod on the back of the bumper car. Sure enough, blue sparks jumped between the rod's tail and the ceiling netting.

He heard the helicopter approaching fast. He heard the wind roar through the alleys between buildings, creating an eerie howl across the pier. He saw the rain begin to change direction from the helicopter's powerfully whirling blades. Then he heard the telltale swoosh of the aircraft clearing the roller-rink wall. The thing should be either right beside the bumper-car building or right overhead.

Brett took the long wooden scabbard for his *katana*, and reached over and placed the tip under the dead man's elbow. Then, with a strong, sharp slash, he pushed the arms up so the tip of the blade hit the metal grating above. The electrical power above surged down the blade and through the effective conductor of flesh, bone, and blood. The water around the corpse's feet was the finishing touch.

The man fried, sending sparks and little bolts of lightning everywhere. The connection was too much for the building's old wiring and generator to bear. All of it blew out, plunging the building into darkness.

Brett cleared the metal floor in one jump, grabbing his sword as he passed the burning body. It was back in its scabbard almost none the worse for wear save for a thin sheet of carbon across it as Brett dove to the ground. He landed just beyond another dead man. When he rolled to his feet, the killer's pistol was in his hand and pointing right up at the hovering helicopter and its confused occupants.

The spotlight wasn't pointing in Brett's direction, but it shed enough light to illuminate the pair in the cockpit. With unerring accuracy, Brett shot the man with the gun through the open side of the helicopter's bubble. The man's seat belt kept him in the aircraft, but it couldn't keep the powerful machine gun in. The Wilkinson carbine slipped from the man's dead fingers and fell to the pier.

The pilot desperately whirled the hovering copter in that direction and wrenched the spotlight down to illuminate the spot where the gun had fallen. Standing in the circle of light was a figure dressed all in black, the dark "Terry" carbine blending in with his shirt. The pilot was helpless to do anything but watch as the Ninja Master opened fire on his craft.

The 9mm bullets smashed through the bubble, careened off the two copter blades and ripped across the framework toward the gas tank. But by then the pilot was already dead. He slumped over, the controls falling from his slack hands. The helicopter spun in place, then dropped. It smashed into the roller-rink roof at the same moment it exploded into flames. Hunks of metal and plastic spread out to crash into the bumper-car building and fall, sizzling, into the sea.

Its raging destruction drowned out any other sound for close to a minute. It slipped off the rink structure lethargically, one of its landing legs catching on a corner so that it tipped over onto its side. Its still-whirling blades hit the pier first, breaking and spinning in all directions with devastating speed. Then the main copter body hit, flattening and smashing the charred corpses in the destroyed cockpit seats.

Even with the rain, the oil fire ignited both the roller-rink and bumper-car buildings, adding a new light to the Atlantic City sky.

More angry than satisfied, Brett threw down the empty Wilkinson weapon and turned back toward the mainland. He had taken refuge behind the bumper-car building—away from the flaming, crashing wreck. He was pleased at the ease of bringing the metal bird down, but angry that it was even there in the first place. He couldn't understand why Arrow would go to such lengths to make sure Shack Sullivan was dead.

Turning his mind away from the copter and the bumper cars, Brett set his gaze on the darkened end of the pier where it attached itself to the Boardwalk and Atlantic City. Suddenly he realized that something was blocking his

*142*

vision. Something was obliterating the end of the pier. A thick, dark line was stretched across the mouth of the wharf. A second later that line took shape when six pairs of headlights clicked into life. Brett was faced with a half-dozen large dark sedans.

A second after their headlights went on, their engines roared. A second after that, the night was filled with the squealing of rubber. The six heavy vehicles tore down the wooden planking toward the Ninja Master.

The thorough ambushing of a single hit man had suddenly turned into an illogical, impractical, and thoroughly insane act. Arrow didn't want Sullivan killed. He wanted him eradicated and he wasn't taking a single chance in the world. The cars jumped forward, rocking on their shocks.

Even with a fully loaded Wilkinson, Brett wasn't sure if he could peg every driver from his angle and still dodge the oncoming cars. Since the Wilkinson's clip was empty, it was a moot point. And there wasn't very much two swords and some *shuriken* could do against the tons of Detroit steel aimed at him. If the element of surprise was on his side, Brett might have been able to kill all the drivers silently, but being pegged in twelve headlight beams blew his cover all to hell.

Brett knew his rear exit was blocked by the flaming helicopter. The cars had already traveled far enough to block all the side exits Brett could have slipped into. He had two choices. One, he could run to the side anyway and try to blast through a wooden door or wall. Or, two, he could use the art of *kyojutsu*. He could do the totally unexpected.

To everyone's surprise, Brett ran forward, directly at the line of cars. In response, the line closed ranks, giving him absolutely no room to snake between two vehicles. He heard the sound of rending metal and complaining tires as the headlights blended together and filled his vision.

Then, when it seemed absolutely certain that he would be hit, Brett leaped into the air—over the speeding cars.

The blinding headlights disappeared as he soared upward, replaced by the calm night sky and the colors of the Boardwalk casinos. Brett heard the angry roar of the autos below, deprived of their seemingly easy victim. Then, at the apex of his leap, another unnatural voice was added to the symphony of deadly sound. From his left, the unmistakable report of a sawed-off double-barreled shotgun tore through the evening dark.

It was only by the purest chance that the pellets hit Brett. It was an even gamble as to whether the cloud of spreading shot would catch him in midflight. But the Mob man had lucked out. Even hanging out the passenger window of the last car on the left and firing at a dark, moving target, some of the lead reached its mark.

Brett tried twisting away from the shot, but there was only so far he could dodge and the pellets spread out. He felt them burrow into his shoulder and across his back with stinging pain. The shock to his nervous system threw off his landing. He just barely hit the ground with his feet and then, rather than somersaulting, he fell and rolled to the side of the nearest building.

He tried to readjust to the new situation as he heard the car brake tortuously. He looked up to see the big sedans screeching around in rough hundred-and-eighty-degree circles. They smashed into their accompanying vehicles' front and rear ends as they tried to turn in the limited area. As they limped around, some passenger doors opened and shotgun-wielding aides jumped out. Brett heard the clank of a pump being pulled back to shove a new shell into the weapon's chamber even as he was bringing up the third of his four *shurikens*. Lying flat on his back, he sent the sharp-edged star into the forehead of the man who had originally shot him.

144

The man with half a metal star sticking out his brow fell back against the wall across the pier as two of the cars finally made it all the way around. Brett managed a painful back-flip to blend in with the shadows along his side. He ran and jumped toward the Boardwalk to avoid being wherever the other men were shooting. He heard their shotguns blast away and the little balls perforating the fronts of the amusement properties.

Brett headed for an alleyway to his right. If he could slip through it, he might be able to jump into the ocean and escape. But just as he moved into the mouth of the alley, he heard the squealing tires of the car nearest him and then the rending, cracking crash of the car colliding with the building to his right. He was forced back as the auto barreled through the old, rotting wall of the structure and kept going until it smashed through the second wall and appeared in the alleyway.

Hunks of wood were thrown up to ricochet off the facing wall. As soon as the driver had braked the car to a halt, he leaned out his open window with a .45 automatic, blasting away at anything he thought might be Brett's retreating figure. Only Brett wasn't about to retreat back onto a road littered with kamikaze cars and frenetic hit men. Keeping well into the shadows on the right, Brett charged the car. He leaped up onto its ceiling silently, whipping out his *katana*. In the same motion as drawing out the sword, he sliced a four-foot-long gash in the car roof.

He did it so fast that by the time the car's two occupants looked, the sword was withdrawn. But it had served its purpose; it had drawn their attention to the ceiling of their car. Brett dropped to the ground just outside the driver's open window and with a straight thrust sent his two-foot-long blade through both the driver's and passenger's head. The blade entered the back of the driver's

145

skull, erupted from his mouth, and entered the passenger's eye to exit from his ear.

Brett pulled the sword loose, and ran into the building through the hole the auto had made. He was spotted by two more shotgun men who were investigating the hole in the front wall. They saw his figure spotlighted in the hole and fired as he dived to the side. Their shots flecked the edges of the hole and blew in the rear windshield of the stalled car. Afraid that they may have hit their own men— not knowing that Brett had already killed them—they moved forward.

The Ninja Master came up from the side, slicing across the back of his first man's neck, severing his spinal cord, and chopping off the second man's gun arm as the mobster tried to dodge out of the way. Brett kept moving out of the hole and into the street as the second man stumbled back, his shoulder stump pumping blood.

The surviving seven hit men spotted Brett's hasty reentry onto the street and scrambled toward him. Three cars careened off each other trying to turn again as Brett raced toward the end of the pier. The Ninja Master showed himself to another gun man across the way so that he'd bring his shotgun to bear. Brett led the killer on, attracting the barrel of the gun to him like a heat-seeking missile onto a bonfire.

At the last second before the Mob man pulled the trigger, thinking he had Brett in the clear, the ninja ducked down. The killer compensated and fired, not realizing that Brett had positioned himself so that a hastily turning car was between him and the gun. The gangster blasted the back of two of his companions' heads. The driver slumped over on the wheel, a car horn adding to the chaos of noise.

Another car got itself turned around again as Brett broke into the clear and started zigzagging toward the still burning helicopter. The driver had the black-garbed figure pinned in his headlights as he pushed the gas pedal to the floor and hunched over the wheel. Brett veered to the right and jumped right into the merry-go-round, clearing a row of three horses. The car plowed right in after him, sending plaster and wood flying and bending metal with an awesome screech.

The circular structure tipped crazily just as Brett emerged from the other side and kept running. The car jumped onto the merry-go-round proper and tried to force its way all the way through. The broken horses and their moorings took their revenge by blasting the tires flat with sharp surfaces and catching the car in a net of twisting poles.

The last three autos finally got themselves facing the right way and gave chase. Brett headed straight for the copter bonfire. Its fury and the rain had served to diminish the flames' height, but the tips of the orange and black heat still reached ten feet. Brett took two preparatory steps toward it and leaped. His shoulder seemed to scream its disapproval as he soared over the flames. There was a wrenching pain which Brett hastily controlled as the fire licked at his feet.

Again he landed imperfectly, sliding onto his side and rolling toward the edge of the pier. As he spun across the ground the saw the cars blast across, through, and over the flaming copter wreckage, spreading it out on their front grills. They burst through the bonfire without slowing down and sped right at his tumbling figure.

Brett threw himself forward into a rolling position. He somersaulted toward the edge, with each turn tearing at his wounded shoulder. He ignored the oncoming cars and the increasing thunder of their engines, concentrating instead on his own speed. It seemed as if he were spinning for minutes rather than just a few seconds. In those moments, he found himself staring at his left shoulder. He saw that the black shirt was completely soaked in blood.

Then there was nothing but air for him to roll on. He

spun down through the warm night air. He turned his body into a spear and plunged into the ocean feet first so his shoulder wouldn't take the brunt of the water's blow.

The cars on the edge of the pier stopped. Four men got out and dotted the surface of the sea with gunfire for a minute, but Brett never surfaced.

After about five minutes checking the ocean's surface, they picked up their wounded and left.

# Chapter Seven

Brett Wallace lay on his back on the ocean floor watching thin, little spirals of blood rise up toward the Atlantic's surface. He saw it as if it were a red ribbon blowing across some rippled, opaque blue-green glass with a dim light behind it. Outside this core of red, blue, and green were only deepening shades of gray and black. He lay on the sandy mud, bled, and didn't breathe.

There was an art in everything, he remembered, even this. *Suiei-jutsu;* the art of underwater survival. Controlling one's breath, pulse, and heartbeat was just part of the art which included swimming and fighting, in, on, or under water. Even wounded and light-headed, he had been such a master of the ninja training that his instincts automatically took over.

Brett lay, blinked, and let the current drag him while

he thought. Something had gone horribly wrong. He had sought to kill Arrow, but Arrow had set a multileveled trap for him that exceeded his expectations for viciousness. The hit men had a backup and the backup had a backup. Lookouts for him were inside the amusement center, on the next pier, and on the shore. If Arrow had arranged to box him in with a boat, Brett would probably be dead.

Instead he was bleeding and rapidly running out of useable oxygen on the ocean bottom. Still the questions remained: how and why? Why did Arrow set him up and how did he know that Brett would be so tough to kill? There were several possible answers for both, but they all held less water than Brett did. First, Arrow could have wanted to kill him because he still didn't trust him and worried about his prowess. He could have set up the ambush because a traitor in Testi's organization had talked. But only Testi and Schonberger knew about the hit. At least those were the only ones Brett knew. Testi could have told someone after Brett left.

Second, Arrow might have set up such a devastating task force simply because he was paranoid about Brett escaping and had magnified Shack Sullivan's feats in his mind. Or the traitor could have informed Arrow about all Sullivan's feats in conjuction with Schonberger's supposed "killing." Or Arrow could've seen Schonberger himself somewhere, tipping him off that Shack hadn't done the job he was supposed to.

Or perhaps Arrow hadn't set him up. Perhaps Testi had gotten wind of the Million Dollar Pier meeting, set up the ambush himself, and caught Brett in it. Maybe all the Arrow men were already dead and Testi didn't want to pay Sullivan the hundred grand he promised. Brett stopped thinking about it when he realized some brain cells were beginning to die from lack of oxygen. The Ninja Master let his body rise. He came up under the pier, between the piles. Then slowly, gingerly, he pushed himself toward shore.

Aaron Schonberger got off the phone and rose from his desk. Surveying the paperwork which he had put into three neat piles on his blotter, he decided it was a fine day with a job well done. He had already transferred the initial fifty-thousand-dollar payment into Shack Sullivan's secret account, but that was all right. According to Testi, they could take it out again the next day. Given the changing situation and tonight's meeting, Sullivan's services would no longer be required.

The money man smiled benevolently at his intricate economic work, then spun to his hat rack. He shrugged on his double knit overcoat, and pulled on his blue, thin-brimmed fedora with the feather in the band. He absent-mindedly rubbed his mustache, tapped his desk top, moved around it and walked to the door. Without looking back, he switched out the light.

It was a wonderful night, Schonberger thought as he passed the hallway leading to John Testi's office. The door was open and the chair behind the huge desk was empty. He had to be on his way to the meeting, Schonberger decided. The thought filled him with renewed pleasure. After all these months, the end of the war was finally in sight. Finally, things would be getting back to their quiet, well-organized norm.

Schonberger went into the cement chamber where the man behind the camera console identified him and opened the second door into the casino. The money man went out and walked behind all the cashiers, bidding them a pleasant evening as he went.

One particularly tired woman, who was serving a double shift to cover for a friend reminded him with a wan smile that they worked until six o'clock in the morning. Schonberger patted her on the shoulder and said, "Well, have the best morning you can, then." He went out the side door and started making his way across the casino floor.

He had just passed the crowded craps table line when a green-sleeved arm disengaged itself from the usual throng of gamblers and settled on Schonberger's shoulder.

Suddenly the money man felt a paralyzing pain spreading across his limbs like lightning. His vocal cords as well as the rest of his muscles were frozen. Another hand came to rest on his other shoulder and easily guided him to one of the tables. The hands edged him between the noisy group cheering a big winner on a roll. Schonberger wound up looking into the placid face of Shack Sullivan.

Only somehow it wasn't Sullivan anymore. He didn't hold himself the same, his manner wasn't the same, and he didn't even look the same in a strange way. Although the face and body was undeniably that of Shack Sullivan, if someone had asked him to be absolutely sure, he would have to say no. It was the same shell but it was not the same man.

Sullivan—or someone else—kept one hand on Schonberger's shoulder, making it look as if he were being particularly friendly. In reality, he was maintaining the paralyzing nerve pinch.

"Where's Testi?" said this Shack Sullivan clone in a quiet voice. The voice had a fascinating edge to it. Although Schonberger heard it clearly, he was sure no one else did. In fact, when the man spoke, all the other voices in the casino became a blurred sound. Only this man's words were clear.

"Didn't John call you?" Schonberger started in surprise. One second of shoulder pressure convinced him to continue in a more sedate fashion. "He said he would get in touch with you. He said it would be all right."

"Get in touch with me?" the Sullivan-like man said, blurring out the voices again. "What for?"

"The meeting," Schonberger explained. At that moment the big roller threw a seven. The crowd around the two men cheered. Their sound was lost amid the conglomerate din going up all over the cavernous room.

"What meeting?" Sullivan asked, bringing Schonberger's attention back to the subject.

"The . . . peace talks," the money man elaborated. "The morning after Testi made the deal with you he got the offer of peace talks with Arrow. Mr. Testi was convinced that Arrow was sincere, so they arranged to talk at midnight over at the Diamond Head."

"The Diamond Head!" Sullivan repeated incredulously. "Is Testi out of his mind?"

"I wondered about that too," Schonberger said honestly. Even if he wasn't such an honest man inherently, the hand squeezing his shoulder kept him honest. "We all did, but John was sure it was on the level. He said it was arranged for the main casino. At this time of night, that's crawling with innocent bystanders. There's no way anyone will start shooting with that many people around."

The Sullivan man was no longer looking into Schonberger's face. He was staring over his shoulder visualizing something other than the Gold Rush casino room.

"Mr. Sullivan?" Schonberger asked. He had to repeat the name twice more before the man responded. He looked at the money man with tired eyes. "Are you all right? You look a bit pale."

"Did you put the fifty thousand where I asked you to?" was the way Sullivan replied.

"Yes," said the money man, but still feeling the throbbing pain in his shoulder underneath the man's fingers, he added, "But Mr. Testi said I could take it back out tomorrow. He said you wouldn't mind."

The Sullivan-like man continued to look at Schonberger. With a weary nod, he closed his eyes. Then he let go of the money man and drifted away from the table. The crowd

suddenly groaned behind Schonberger. The Mob econo-
mist turned to see that the big winner had just crapped
out. When he turned back, Shack Sullivan was gone, completely gone. No matter how hard or much he looked
through the crowd, Schonberger could not see hide nor
hair of him. The pain in his shoulder was completely gone
as well as was any stiffness in his limbs. It was as if Sullivan had never appeared and the conversation had not
taken place.

But as soon as Schonberger had decided that it was all
a daydream or nightmare, he caught sight of something
on the floor at his feet. Between the many other shoes, he
saw a small dot. Taking his life in his hands because of
all the trampling legs in the area, the money man leaned
over and put his finger on the dot. It was wet and it came
away red. Schonberger rubbed the liquid between his
finger and thumb. The money man recognized it easily. It
was blood.

Members of the Gold Rush staff would later find errant
drops of blood in the casino and across the lobby. People
on the street would walk over other drops, not seeing them
for all the other stains on the sidewalk. But if all the drops
were connected like a giant connect-the-dots game, a line
would be made from the Gold Rush to the Diamond Head
casino-hotel. Only the line would not go inside. It would
abruptly stop and start around the outside. Then it would
stop completely.

Brett Wallace put the finishing touches on his second
tourniquet and bandage in the Gold Rush bushes along the
side wall. With the shotgun wounds stretching across one
side of his back, it had been hard for him to cover every
cut. But finally he got every hole covered to the best of
his ability and satisfaction.

He had taken off the first bandage, made up of his ninja

154

uniform and created this new one from the clothes of the dead guard he had found in the bushes earlier.

This security man, dumped in an obscure spot away from the crowds, was but the first Brett was sure he'd find scattered inside and out Arrow's establishment. Once he had found the corpse, he had finally put together the only possible truth of the cross and double-cross Mob war. He had put together an incredible but plausible plot that explained everyone's actions and his own injury. He had put together a story that left him tired and bitter.

If the peace talks were not being held in a public place where innocent people, contrary to what Schonberger thought, were destined to get hurt, Brett would have held back and let the plot go forward, so all he'd have to do was mop up afterward. But the brain behind the war was cunning and ruthless. Ruthless enough to sacrifice anyone —connected or unconnected—to gain control of all the Atlantic City vices.

Brett put his green shirt back on over the bandage and tucked it into his brown slacks. He buried his blood-soaked uniform and retrieved his swords. He stood and climbed out of the foliage. Taking only his sash from his now useless *shinobi shozoko,* he placed the swords inside and moved toward the rear of the establishment.

On the rear wall was a service and kitchen door. Brett waited several minutes to see what kind of activity went on inside. During the time he was waiting, only a chef's helper appeared outside to throw away some garbage. Brett checked his internal clock. It was very near midnight. Any change of staff would have been completed. He moved silently and sideways toward the service entrance.

Even before he got there, he knew it was locked. With a quick twist of his wrist and the flicking of two fingers, he brought the lock-pick up into his palm from its wire holder on his wrist. It was one of the few things he had in his duffel bag beside the *shuko* tiger claws. Without lean-

155

ing over, Brett noiselessly unlocked the metal partition. But before he swung it open, he put the flat of all ten fingers against it. There was slight movement inside. It was a still but tense movement. He heard fast, muffled breathing. Someone was waiting inside and that someone was nervous.

Brett pulled back the door so there was no sound of it opening, then he slipped in just as soundlessly. By the time the masked hit man noticed that someone had come in, Brett had already pulled his *wakizashi* from its scabbard and thrown it like a spear down the concrete entry hall. The blade went right through the hit man's chest.

He gurgled, grabbed the blade with one hand, and tried to bring up his silenced automatic with his other. But as his gloved fingers closed on the short samurai blade, it cut through the leather like a laser through paper and chopped off two of his fingers. The other fingers stopped halfway cut through. Before the man could scream through his brown ski-mask, he died. He fell back, hit the wall, and slid down to a sitting posture on the floor. Brett walked up, seeing the murdered desk man slumped over onto the entry table. The hit man must have killed him and remained to do the same to any one coming in curious or late. This was a vicious group, willing to kill any witnesses whether they could identify them or not.

Brett pulled his short sword out, wiped it on the dead man's shirt and put it back into its holder as he approached the stairway to the left of the entry office. Speed and thoroughness were the watchwords now. He had to survey and control the scene before any more innocents could get hurt, but he had to do it in such a way that he wouldn't be killed. His shoulder's throbbing had been pushed so far back into his mind that it felt like a distant pulse.

He looked up the steps. They went straight up, ending at the third floor, without any turns. There was one level on the second floor. At that point, the gray, plain walls of the entry hall and office turned into the plush scarlet wallpaper and carpet of the Diamond Head decor. There were only three sources of illumination in this stairwell: that of the cellar hallway, one bulb over the second floor landing, and a dim red light coming from around the corner on the third floor.

Brett moved up the steps, keeping well to the right. He was calm, but his soul was not at peace. He was just tidying up after the mess had been made. He was just trying to prevent a bigger mess. As he neared the top of the stairs, all his senses were at their fullest.

He heard the muffled roar of the casino at its peak. He heard the cries of winners and the groans of losers. He felt the intensity of hundreds of hungry people. People who wanted, begged, hoped, pleaded, and prayed to win any amount, any amount at all. And once that was over, they would start over again.

Over that he felt the intensity of several more people. Distant people, detached from the throng. Their concentration was centered on something else beside winning money. Brett heard their breathing. Four sets of inhalations and exhalations. Slow, deep, steady, and conscious breaths—closer than the frenetic gasps of the gamblers. These four were on a totally different plateau than the gamblers, both mentally and physically.

Brett stepped onto the third-story platform. As he looked to the right, he saw it wasn't so much the third story as a mezzanine over the second floor. And since the service entrance was in a sublevel, he was now standing on a platform above the first floor proper of the Diamond Head establishment. To his right was a long floor section which reached to the opposite wall and the entrance to several catwalks attached to it.

The Diamond Head, like the Gold Rush and all the others, had a secret section above the main floor of the

157

casino where guards watched the patrons and the dealers to make sure everything was as it should be. Brett was standing to the left of that. A wall blocked his view of the guards and vice versa. Only he was sure the Diamond Head guards were no longer in charge.

Since the four men Brett had sensed up here were depending on the dead hit man downstairs to guard them, Brett figured all their concentration would be centered on their targets. So the Ninja Master cautiously pushed his head around the corner just far enough to see. A second later his head was back completely. He had burned the scene into his mind.

Six men; two dead. The four others were kneeling and lying on the catwalk, snipers' rifles attached to the floor or railings by vise clamps. Two men were stationed on the near catwalk, two men stationed on the far catwalk. Each man was aiming at one of two different targets with one of two different guns. Each man at each station was aiming at a different target, so if he missed, he'd be backed up by the man at the other station. And at each station there was a silenced 7.62 MZI sniper's rifle and the 7.62 Spartco silenced single-shot model. All these men needed was one shot and then they'd be gone. The real danger to the public was down below.

Brett could picture it. George Arrow and John Testi seated across a private table, playing cards among the throng. To chase away an audience and add that extra measure of security was one bodyguard each—their best men—standing behind their respective bosses. When the two Mob leaders were killed from above, they would be hard pressed not to start shooting at each other. And in that chaos, the real killers would escape and some tourists might be shot or trampled in the rush for the exits.

Brett leaned up against the protecting wall with his back. He reached in to the pouch on his belt and brought up his last poison-coated *shuriken*. His pouch was waterproof so his little dip in the sea had not washed the lethal factor off. Still, he would have to throw it perfectly. He leaned over and looked at his four targets again.

The dead duo were dressed in Diamond Head uniforms. The two pairs of killers were dressed like their skewered companion downstairs, in dark clothes and ski masks, only their masks were pulled off their heads and littering the floor. At this point they thought themselves safe from recognition. After all, a two-way mirror was between them and the revelers below. They could see the gamblers, but the gamblers could only see themselves if they looked up.

The four were positioned in such a way that Brett couldn't cut them all no matter how much of a curve he put on the throwing star. He would have to be satisfied with two, leaving the other pair to his more personal attention. The important thing was not to let them kill the mob leaders. That would be the guards' cue to open up. So the *shuriken* would have to take out the men farthest from him.

Brett prepared himself. He moved to the side, toward the infrared light which covered the room and kept those below ignorant of those above. Brett took the one lone *shuriken* and brought it back with his right hand. His left hand rested on his sword hilts. He placed the lying and kneeling figures in his mind. He pictured all the possibilities resulting from his actions. He prepared himself for any one of them. He channeled all his energy toward his right hand. Without any more conscious thought, he brought the sharp throwing star around the corner at a dizzying speed.

The *shuriken* left his hand and streaked across the room as Brett leaped into the air. The star ripped across the back of the farthest lying man—tearing open his shirt and making a six-inch gash across his skin—before flattening out and slicing through the kneeling man's pants cuff and drawing a drooling red line across his ankle. Brett had thrown it so hard and so fast that the men didn't know they were cut until a second after the whirling blade thudded into the opposite wall. And by then it was too late. Their fingers grew slack on the triggers and they lost consciousness. They died a second after that, the kneeling man tipping over.

As Brett reached the peak of his jump, both blades flashed out, the *wakizashi* in his left hand and the *katana* in his right. The blades were not spun toward the final two assassins, they were aimed for the guns. Just as the men became aware of the flying figure, his blades lashed forward, pushing the guns away from their targets. Taken by surprise, the hit men couldn't help but pull their triggers. The bullets smashed into the mezzanine wall and Brett landed on the catwalk in front of them.

His hands moved forward again. The long sword in his right hand snaked by the kneeling man and drove through the prone assassin. The short blade in his left hand moved too, but, incredibly, missed its target. An accident and Brett's wound conspired to throw him off. The kneeling man had lunged back when Brett had deflected his aim, rising to his feet and taking the gun—vise and all—with him. When Brett thrust upon landing, the now standing man dodged, tripping over the lying guy and completely falling out of Brett's kill zone.

Brett stumbled off balance too, his shoulder twisting painfully. He knew at once that he was bleeding again. In anger, he jabbed the short sword at the only remaining hit man again. Out of pure luck and desperation, the guy managed to parry it with his rifle. Totally fed up, Brett brought his *katana* slashing from the side with his strong right arm. The blade sliced completely through the thickest part of the gun, metal and all. The rifle was cut clean in two pieces.

Stunned, the man dropped the two pieces. He stared with bulging eyes at Brett. They stood facing each other, leaning on either side of the catwalk. Something about the man's stare stopped Brett cold. He had seen the expression before. It was the look of a man seeing death. In a moment, Brett understood why. The man's hands reached toward his throat. Just before the fingers covered his neck, Brett saw a flap of skin fall away and a spitting cloud of blood erupt. He had been so inaccurate in his sword thrusts that he had not only chopped the gun in half, he had sliced open the man's throat behind it.

The hit man tried to stem the tidal wave of crimson with his strong fingers, but it didn't work. The liquid bubbled around his hands, turning his front into a sodden scarlet mess in seconds. As Brett watched, the man fell back, seemingly in slow motion, over the catwalk's protecting guard rail.

The ninja finally snapped out of his emotional spell and hurled himself across the platform to see the last hit man float down to the glass ceiling of the casino and smash right through.

An entire section of the casino roof blasted outward and down in the company of a blood-soaked, still-living man. He slammed down onto the table separating George Arrow from John Testi.

Brett reacted immediately. The guards were already going for their guns when Brett hurled both his swords downward, one in each hand. The blade tips entered each standing guard's head at the same time and drove down until only the hilts protruded from their hair. Only Arrow's guard was fast enough to grab his gun before he died. Still in its holster, he unconsciously shot himself in the foot before he fell over.

As Brett threw his swords and the last hit man landed, John Testi rose. He had started to get up the moment the roof started splitting open. He was prepared for a double cross of any kind. Right after his blades had left his hands, Brett watched as Testi pointed his metal wrist stump at

Arrow. Arrow tried to get up, his hands tightening on the arms of his chair as the last of the broken glass fell about his head.

Testi ignored the shards which bounced off his scalp and broad shoulders. A smoking hole suddenly appeared in his shirtsleeve and a little red fountain was spurting between Arrow's eyes. The squat Mob boss sat down heavily, his hands turning white on the chair arms. His eyes remained opened as he slumped and Testi turned hurriedly away.

Brett vaulted the catwalk railing and dropped down onto the table, his feet straddling the last hit man's corpse. The room had turned into the madhouse the ninja had feared. People were screaming and crawling over each other to get out. But through them all plowed John Testi. He would wrench anyone out of his way with massive sweeps of his real hand as well as his hook.

"Testi!" Brett shouted after him, his voice carrying over the shouts of the hundreds collected there. The remaining Mob boss turned long enough to fire another shot from the gun installed behind his hook. It was just like the one famed handless detective J. J. Armes had—a weapon actually attached to his arm's nerve endings so he could fire it by thought alone.

Brett didn't bother to duck. He knew the bullet would miss him by three inches. But the second shot only stirred up the hysteria more. People peeled away from Testi like nuns from a skunk.

"Testi!" Brett shouted again. "Don't!" It was all he could think of saying.

The Mob boss misunderstood. He thought Brett was planning to kill him, so he plowed through the mob even faster than before. He didn't know that Brett was trying to save him.

The Ninja Master considered picking up a handful of glass or heavy, thick poker chips to hurl at Testi, but he thought better of it, given his weakened left arm and the undulating crowd of innocents being tossed back in his wake. With slow, deliberate movements, Brett leaned down and pulled his swords out of the guards' skulls. He flicked them down to throw the blood off, then slipped them back into their scabbards. He watched as Testi managed to ram his way out the exit doors and the casino security guards began to break through the crowd in the other direction.

Brett leaped nimbly up to the catwalk again. His jump brought his hands high enough to grab the railing, then he vaulted up and over onto the suspended floor. From there he jumped to the landing. From there he took the stairway in two more jumps. He ran down the hall and burst out the back door ten seconds before the first hotel employee could reach it. By the time that employee had gone inside and discovered the other corpses, Brett was well on his way back to the Gold Rush.

By the time he got to the Gold Rush, the crowds were being emptied out and the cops had already been called. Brett made his way through the throng of curious on-lookers until he sidled up to a chubby youth with a beard. "What's going on?" he asked.

The fellow didn't even notice Brett's swords. In fact, he didn't even look at Brett. His eyes were glued to the Gold Rush entrance.

"I don't know," the youth said at first, then immediately made himself a liar. "Somebody went crazy with a machine gun inside or something."

Brett moved away from the escaping guests and the thrill seekers to move in the same way he gained entry to the Diamond Head. He found the employee's section empty. He found the elevator—no stairway—to the cat-walk above the casino and found that devoid of life as well. Walking on the suspended platform, he saw that the casino looked as if a tornado had hit it. He imagined that it was exactly what the Diamond Head would look like after it was emptied.

Tables were overturned, chips were strewn everywhere, broken glass, broken furniture, enough paper to supply a ticker-tape parade and several shoes. It looked like a ghost casino. Half the lights were out, throwing the large room into a dank dimness. It brought to mind the feeling one got in the back of the throat after losing more than he could afford.

Brett hopped over the railing and crashed through the two way mirrored ceiling. He landed on the floor between table rows, flipped, and came up facing the last cashier's booth. On the back wall of the booth were several dripping patches of blood. Next to those was the open door of the vacuum room. The sliding metal door beyond that was open as well. Then he heard a groaning from behind the desk.

Brett trotted over and vaulted over the cashier counter. Lying up against the wall was Aaron Schonberger, his chest drilled. He was very dead. The groaner was the girl who had been staffing the cashier post earlier in the evening. While the money man had gotten it full in the torso, she had part of her shoulder and arm ripped off. She had been sliding in circles in a pool of her own and Schonberger's blood. Brett put her to sleep with acupressure. He wasn't sure if she would ever wake up, but if not, then at least she would die in peace.

Taking no chances, Brett leaped through the tiny reinforced concrete and iron room. He didn't want to be caught in there again. He made his way cautiously through Testi's office complex, bringing all his sensory powers to bear. As he snaked through he felt the presence of almost no one. But as he drew near Testi's office, the evidence of living things grew stronger. There was disruptive energy within the complex. Not much, but some. There were snatches of breath he could pick up, then they would fuzz out.

All the sensory information centered on Testi's office. Looking down his hall, Brett could see the door to the main room ajar. Behind it were all the feelings he had felt on the Million Dollar Pier. There were energy spirits taunting him. There were demons of his own mind and those of others laughing at him, egging him on. He walked down the hall, heading for the open door purposefully. Whatever the outcome, it would end here.

He stopped in front of the partition and pushed open the door.

Behind it, John Testi sat in his darkened office, behind his huge desk, his metal arm on the table top, pointing at the door. The hook was gone and the knife was in its place.

His eyes were open, but Brett knew he was dead. His chest didn't move, his nostrils didn't flare, there was no subtle but necessary movement of his veins anywhere on his body. His neck, wrist, and forehead didn't minutely throb with the coursing of blood. Brett pulled his swords from his sash and approached the desk. He laid his blades on the opposite end of the table from Testi's pointing knife.

That's when he heard the click. His head moved in the direction it came from, rather than dodging or dropping. So he was not prepared when Testi's arm blew off.

The joint between his artificial limb and his upper arm actually exploded, sending out little chunks of flesh and steel while propelling the metal arm forward like a rocket. The concussion was enough to throw Brett back, but his balance was disturbed enough so that he couldn't avoid the flying arm. He instinctively chopped down with his good right arm, preventing the blade from sinking into his stomach as he fell back, but he couldn't keep the blasted end of the arm from snapping up into his face.

He was blinded and stunned for a second, then he felt the plush carpet on his back and heard the merry tinkle of a female laugh. He sat up and saw Tamara, Arrow's girl friend, standing beside Testi's ravaged body with a small remote control box in one hand and Brett's swords in the other.

When she stopped laughing, she said, "It's really very easy. You just unstrap the arm and put a small plastic explosive charge in instead of three bullets. Then you just press this little button and boom." She laughed again. "Both Testi and my George really liked their gadgets," she sighed.

"You were the traitor in Arrow's organization," Brett gasped.

"Oh, I don't like the label 'traitor,' " the beautiful blond pouted. "I would prefer something like 'executive information source.' Or 'crisis catalyst,' or something like that. After all, it was me who got Georgie all hot under the collar about you. I told him you came on to me and wouldn't take no for an answer. That's why he tried to hack you into little pieces at the pier."

"That wasn't the only reason," Brett added, rising from the floor to stand in place.

"Of course not, silly," Tamara chirped. "He had to kill you to protect himself, but we wanted to make sure he did the job right so we added the little white frosting."

"We?" Brett echoed.

"Of course we," the blond reiterated. "But I'll bet you know all about that by now. That's why you're here, isn't it?"

Brett nodded.

"Too bad," said Tamara. "It's really too bad you got in the way, Mr.—just who are you, anyway?"

"I am no one," Brett said lightly but not without conviction.

Tamara shrugged. "Have it your way. Whoever you are, you're mighty tough to kill. All those hit men, all that planning, all that thinking and still we just can't seem to get a bullet between your eyes." On that word, Tamara put the remote control box down and came up with a Walther automatic.

Brett raised his eyebrows at her choice of gun.

"Oh, I know more than guns, Mr. No One," she assured him. "Why do you think I became friends with Mr. Georgie Porgie? What do you think I did all day waiting for his call so I could run, all dumb and helpless, to his side? Practice makes perfect, they say. And man, did I practice!" Tamara threw down the long sword on the desk and wrenched the *wakizashi* from its scabbard. She hefted it professionally and swung it a few times. "Jesus," she breathed, "what a beautiful blade!" Then she sliced it violently through the air and right through one of the desk legs. Here was a very strong girl.

"Brand new," she mused, keeping the gun barrel steady on Brett's chest, "but made by the finest Japanese craftsman." She looked directly at Wallace. "You're becoming more interesting by the second, Mr. No One. It's too bad we could not know each other longer."

She pulled the trigger of the Walther practically point blank with it dead center on Brett's chest. She missed.

Brett made her miss. He knew exactly what the Walther was and what it took to fire it. Those long sessions with Hama and in front of the computer screen taught him everything he needed to know about guns. All he needed to know in this case was what type of caliber her Walther was made for: .22LR, .32 ACP, or .380 ACP. If .22, she'd have eight shots fully loaded. The other two clips held seven. There was greater power in the latter two which traveled its 3.86-inch barrel faster. The heft would be slightly more, weighing in at twenty-three-and-a-half ounces with the heavier loads.

Seeing her veins and muscles tense, he simply got out of the way at the right time.

"What the fuck . . ." she exclaimed, pointing the gun at him again. She fired again. It missed again.

Brett ran for the right wall. She fired at him as he went. He didn't stop. He headed right for the curtains that covered the wall. She must have hidden behind them while Brett had approached Testi, he figured, so he wanted to see for himself what was behind them. She came after him, gun pointing. He slapped both palms on the curtains. They billowed back and hit a solid wall. She pulled the trigger, pointing the gun barrel at his back from a distance of ten feet. The bullet went through the curtain and smacked into the wall right next to his moving, dropping neck.

They both ran forward at the same time, Tamara dropping the gun and swinging the short sword. Brett ran from her and smacked one foot flat on the wall. She swung at his torso as his other foot sprang in front of the first. The blade whistled through the air and just missed him as he ran up the office wall.

They both stopped at the same time. Tamara watched, her jaw growing slack. Brett stood, spun, and saw Tamara's head as a beer bottle. His right hand moved, his palm in the *shuto* or knife hand position. Her head cracked open under his assault and his hand sunk into her brain. It didn't quite break through the other side. The human skull is not a glass bottle.

Tamara fell back, a trail of gray and red guts marking her fall. Brett dropped back to the floor on his feet. He collected his blades and left the room.

He found Angelina Arcudi standing in the cashier's booth on the other side of the vacuum room with a gun to Neal Duggan's head. His eyes were red and tearing.

168

"You cry too much, old man," Brett said from his position next to the sliding door.

"I'm sorry," the man said, his voice cracking. "I've been a fool."

"You can say that again," said Angelina, pushing the barrel tighter against his forehead. "Only the word is 'tool.' You've been enormously helpful but I don't need you anymore."

"You don't need anybody anymore, do you, Angel?" Brett inquired. "You used everybody to get what you wanted. And you wanted it all. Like father, like daughter."

"What are you, a cop?" she said in reply.

"I am what I said," Brett answered. "A mercenary with no past."

"And now you got no future," Angelina spat. "Get in the room."

"Why should I?" Brett asked quietly.

"Don't play games!" Angelina yelled, pushing the gun against Duggan's head again. "You know this asshole is innocent as the day is long. And you know if I don't kill him, I'll just kill you, so get into the room!"

Brett seemed to consider it for a minute. His face was expressionless, his eyes veiled. He looked tired—exhausted in fact. He looked like he didn't care any more. Finally he shrugged and stepped into the small concrete enclosure.

Angelina nearly smacked her lips with pleasure. She pulled the remote control box from behind Duggan's back and slammed the cashier's door while automatically sealing the sliding door with the press of a button.

"Think nice thoughts!" she shouted to Brett. "They'll be your last!"

The Ninja Master sat against the wall next to the sliding door. He put his legs out and laid his hands, palm up, at his side. He closed his eyes and thought.

His big mistake, after deciding to avenge Vicki, was

169

looking for victims and villains. There was neither one nor the other. They were all one and the same. He had let himself be sorely used because he was so intent on finding the good guys amid the squabbling bad guys who were only looking out for number one. He was so sure there had to be an innocent caught in the middle that he didn't realize the innocent was himself.

His mind cleared for a second and the image of another innocent took shape. Brett saw the face of Barbara Kelly in his mind's eye. He assuaged himself by realizing that the whole ugly affair did have some purpose after all. By now the prostitute's baby was in San Francisco and the money he had gotten from Arrow and Testi for the hits was being wired over for the little girl's trust fund.

It had been all for her. If Brett had been unable to save the mother from the greedy machinations of Arcudi, at least he was able to give the daughter a chance and new meaning to the elderly life of Diane Kelly. Granddaughter and grandmother would be together. Before stopping Stillman all those days ago, Brett had instructed Rhea to collect the child and arrange for Diane to have custody. Then Brett merely went from one Mob boss to the other, collecting money for hits he never completed. That money went toward Barbara Kelly's future life. Hopefully, she would live a life worthy of the second chance Brett had given her.

Then Angelina pressed the button again and all the air went out of the room with a thunderclap.


"How can you kill him that way?" Duggan wailed, quaking away from the gun.

"The damn guy seems unkillable any other way, old man," Angelina said bluntly. "I wanted to make sure this time." She stood leaning on the cashier's counter across from the blood-flecked door, as Duggan stood to the side between the still corpses of the cashier and Schonberger.

"Do you hate him that much?" the man asked.

"I don't hate him at all," she answered. "He was just a pain in the ass after awhile, that's all. At first, he seemed like he could speed things along a little bit. But then we just couldn't get rid of him.

"He set Testi and Arrow against each other, while Tamara controlled Georgie and I controlled Johnnie."

"He . . . he was in love with you?" Duggan wondered aloud.

"That, or something like it," Angelina explained, the gun loose in her hand. "It was a great system. Testi told me everything, I told Tamara everything, and she told Arrow what we wanted him to hear. We needed a war so there could be peace talks so we could kill them both at once."

"But . . . but you set up your own people!" the old man exclaimed. "You had your own girls executed."

Angelina looked at him very closely. "I'm getting sick of your whining, old man," she said. Then she shot him.

Neal Duggan flew back against the wall, his old heart giving out before the bullet could do the job. He slid down to make a trio with the other two corpses there.

Angelina Arcudi, the new underworld head of Atlantic City, checked her watch. The man who called himself Shack Sullivan had been inside for two minutes. She remembered Testi telling her that he had nearly lost consciousness after three seconds the first time. But this time he had been prepared, so maybe he was holding his breath. Angelina waited some more.

She thought about how good it would be controlling everything. She would run it the way her mother would have, only with an iron hand. The rest of the Mob wouldn't complain because she would make lots of money for them. And God help any of them who tried to steal a little of her thunder. She thought about Tamara. The Sullivan guy must've killed her since he came out and she didn't. Just as well, she figured. The blond bitch probably would've gotten a swelled head that had to be deflated.

She thought about Shack Sullivan. A hell of a guy, if Cyndi was to be believed, with a lot of style and athletic talent. Angelina would never forget when he came roaring through the attic window. And talk about slippery. Even the small army on the pier couldn't get rid of him for good. But there was no ocean inside that room he could escape to.

She checked her watch again. Almost eight more minutes had gone by. She figured she'd better get into the office complex and out the secret escape route before the cops got in.

Angelina pressed the remote control button and broke the seal on the door. Air flushed in, pushing the door open further. She pressed the button again, hearing the sliding door automatically open. She stepped up into the room and began to cross over into the main hallway.

She stopped when she saw Brett Wallace. He was lying with his back up against the wall, his feet and hands straight out on the floor. His head was straight, his eyes were closed and his expression was placid and peaceful.

She couldn't understand it. Wasn't your tongue supposed to stick out, your eyes bulge and your face turn blue when you suffocate, she wondered. Perplexed, and just a little nervous, she approached the man's body.

Kneeling in front of him, she checked his heartbeat by putting her hand against his chest inside his shirt. She couldn't feel anything. She took his wrist between her fingers and felt for a pulse. Nothing. Finally she put her palm against his neck to feel for a pulse there. Absolutely nothing.

She looked up into his calm face in confusion. So she didn't see his hands rise and clamp around her throat.

Brett Wallace surfaced. He rose from the deep sea of

meditation and the art of *suiei-jutsu*. His eyes opened, looking deep into Angelina Arcudi's olive ones. He saw the fear there. He smiled. Then he squeezed.

She died with her tongue out, her eyes bulging, and her face blue.

# 5 EXCITING ADVENTURE SERIES MEN OF ACTION BOOKS

**NINJA MASTER**
*by Wade Barker*
Committed to avenging injustice, Brett Wallace uses the ancient Japanese art of killing as he stalks the evildoers of the world in his mission.
**#3 BORDERLAND OF HELL**                              *(C30-127, $1.95)*

**DIRTY HARRY**
*by Dane Hartman*
The tough, unorthodox plainclothesman of the San Francisco Police Department tackles crimes and violence—nothing can stop him.
**#1 DUEL FOR CANNONS**                              *(C90-793, $1.95)*
**#2 DEATH ON THE DOCKS**                            *(C90-792, $1.95)*
**#3 THE LONG DEATH**                                *(C90-848, $1.95)*

**THE HOOK**
*by Brad Latham*
Gentleman detective, boxing legend, man-about-town, The Hook crosses 1930's America and Europe in pursuit of perpetrators of insurance fraud.
**#1 THE GILDED CANARY**                             *(C90-882, $1.95)*
**#2 SIGHT UNSEEN**                                  *(C90-841, $1.95)*

**S-COM**
*by Steve White*
High adventure with the most effective and notorious band of military mercenaries the world has known—four men and one woman with a perfect track record.
**#2 STARS AND SWASTIKAS**                           *(C90-993, $1.95)*
**#3 THE BATTLE IN BOTSWANA**                        *(C30-134, $1.95)*

**BEN SLAYTON: T-MAN**
*by Buck Sanders*
Based on actual experiences, America's most secret law-enforcement agent—the troubleshooter of the Treasury Department—combats the enemies of national security.
**#1 A CLEAR AND PRESENT DANGER**                    *(C30-020, $1.95)*
**#2 STAR OF EGYPT**                                 *(C30-017, $1.95)*
**#3 THE TRAIL OF THE TWISTED CROSS**                *(C30-131, $1.95)*

# THE BEST OF ADVENTURE
## by RAMSAY THORNE